j398.2   ROSS, Patricia Fent
           In Mexico they say. Illustrated by
           Henry C. Pitz. New York, Knopf, 1942.
Related   211p. illus. 3.00
Books in   *1. Folk-lore, Mexican*
Catalog
Under

           * Fourteen old folk-tales about saints,
             animals, elves, princes and princesses.
             Ages 9 - 12.

                              Title.   D 64

4

IN MEXICO THEY SAY

IN MEXICO
THEY SAY

by Patricia Fent Ross

Illustrated by
HENRY C. PITZ

NEW YORK · ALFRED · A · KNOPF

First Edition April 24, 1942
Second Printing July, 1944
Third Printing September, 1946
Fourth Printing September, 1951
Fifth Printing May, 1956
Sixth Printing August, 1961

THIS IS A BORZOI BOOK

Published by Alfred A. Knopf, Inc.

Copyright 1942 by Alfred A. Knopf, Inc.

FOR

Joan, June, Sheila and Keith
who
first liked these stories

CONTENTS

CONTENTS

IN MEXICO THEY SAY

Salvador and the Goat

ONCE upon a time on a big hacienda in Mexico there lived a little burro named Salvador. When he was a baby burro Salvador thought that life was made up of long sunny roads, and flowering trees, and soft nights when the human people of the hacienda played guitars and sang beautiful songs.

But when he grew up he found that all little burros have work to do, and his work, like that of all the other burros on the hacienda, was to carry loads to town. Sometimes he carried corn, and sometimes he carried wheat, and sometimes he carried grass. But Salvador did not mind at all. He grew accustomed to the load on his back and to the shouts of Miguel, the man who always went to town with the burros.

After all, he was on the long sunny road with all the other burros, and it was fun to see if he could always be just a little bit ahead of the others. They would rest in the town and then at night come back along the long sunny road to the hacienda. Then he and all the other burros ate their sacate, and lay in the moonlight and listened to the people playing guitars and singing beautiful songs. Life was good and he was very happy.

But one day in the town Salvador met a goat named George. Salvador gave George part of his corn and sacate and they sat down to talk.

"They tell me," said George, "that on the hacienda life is very hard. They say the goats must hunt all day on the mountain for grass to eat, and the burros must work all day carrying heavy loads and are always hungry."

"Well, I did not know that," said Salvador, "although I live on the hacienda. It is true that the goats graze on the mountain, but I thought they liked the grass they find there. And it is true that we burros carry heavy loads, and sometimes on the long sunny road we are hungry. But there is always food and rest when we get home. I have always thought it very pleasant on the hacienda, with the moon shining and the people playing guitars and singing beautiful songs." But in spite of his brave words Salvador felt a little troubled.

"Well," said George the Goat, "they tell me that it is a very unpleasant place and that all the animal people there are very unhappy."

"Who tells you?" asked Salvador.

"The coyotes and the zopilotes and the mosquitoes and the fleas, and all the animal people that travel over the world and know everything," said George.

Then Salvador was really troubled. Surely if the coyotes and the zopilotes and all the animal people said this, it must be true. And because he was only a little burro and not very smart, he had never found it out.

But when he walked home along the long sunny road he found it very pleasant. And at night he was so glad to be home at the hacienda again that he ate his corn and sacate and lay down on the soft grass and looked at the little new moon. And then he forgot all about what George had said and went sound asleep.

But he dreamed a dream. In the dream he was walking down the long sunny road, looking at the lovely red and yellow flowers that grew by the path. And a goat came along and ate all the flowers! And although the rains came and the sun shone, no more flowers would grow. He was very sad because he loved the flowers. Then he woke up and knew it was only a dream. But he remembered what George had said to him, and was troubled and unhappy. And so for the rest of the night he did not sleep very well.

The next day as he walked along the sunny road and saw the flowers beside the path, he remembered his dream. And

was still a little troubled. So he hurried up to walk beside
the Oldest Burro, who was very wise and knew everything.
The Oldest Burro had once had a name but everyone had forgotten it, because they all called her Abuela (which is Spanish
for "grandmother").

"Abuela!" said Salvador. "Do you think that life on the
hacienda is very hard?"

"Sometimes," said the Oldest Burro, "when I have a
stomach-ache, or the roads are slippery with rain, and the
load is over-heavy. Then I wish I were a goat, grazing on
the mountain. But usually I am thinking about the corn and
sacate I will have when I get home at night, and how pleasant
it is to lie on the grass and listen to the music. It is the only
life I know, so I am not sure if it is a hard life or not, but I
find it pleasant enough. It is better not to think about it."

Salvador felt that was not a very good answer and he was
still a little troubled. He stopped to snatch a few mouthfuls
of grass, and was very careful not to eat the lovely red and
yellow flowers that grew above the grass.

The next time Salvador saw George in the town, the goat
was very much excited.

"I am surprised to see you," said George. "How did you
happen to escape?"

"I did not escape," said Salvador. "I just walked down the
long sunny road, exactly the same as I do every day."

"And how many of the animal people were killed?" asked
George.

"Killed? None that I know of. I did hear that the human

people at the hacienda killed a sheep last week and ate him. But that is all. How would they be killed?"

"Why, by the earthquake, to be sure! And didn't you know that last night the hacienda was completely destroyed by a terrific earthquake?"

"That is very strange," said Salvador. "I knew nothing about it, for I was sleeping very soundly. And I went to sleep early because the music at the hacienda was particularly beautiful and soothing last night."

"Well," said George, "there was a great earthquake and all the world shook. Here in town we felt it only a little. But they say that at the hacienda the earth opened in great cracks, and all the buildings fell, and the house is a mass of stones, and all the human people are killed, and most of the animal people. And the fields are like great canyons. I am surprised that you were able to walk the long sunny road today, for they say that, too, is like a great canyon. I never expected to see you again!"

"I must be stupid," said Salvador, "for I knew nothing about it. I ate my corn and sacate this morning, the same as usual. And Miguel put the pack on my back and we all came to town down the long sunny road, just as we do every day. I did not see a thing wrong at the hacienda."

"You surely are stupid!" said George. "You don't see what happens right under your nose!" And he snorted and walked away in disgust.

Salvador went home with all the other burros, thinking about what George had said. He thought it very strange that he had noticed nothing, and also strange that all the other burros were not talking about the earthquake. He tried to get Abuela, who was very wise, to tell him about it. But the Oldest Burro was dozing as she walked, and before he could get her to wake up they arrived at the hacienda.

There was the big house that the human people lived in, with the flowers growing in the patio, and the sun making beautiful shadows on the adobe walls, and the birds singing in the trees, exactly as if nothing had happened. Salvador was very much surprised, but he felt better. He was a stupid little burro not to have known about the earthquake, but it seemed that everyone else was just as stupid. The people who were killed, and the animals who were killed, and even the house that had been swallowed up in the earth—none of them, it seemed, knew any more about it than he did. Perhaps he was dead, too, and just did not know it. So he was still a little troubled.

When he lay down to sleep in the moonlight that night, and heard the guitars playing and the people singing beautiful songs up at the big house, it was all very sad because none of them knew about the terrible earthquake.

Even the next day no one knew about it, and Miguel put the packs on the backs of the burros just the same as every day, and they all went to town, down the long sunny road. But Salvador was still troubled. So he walked beside the Oldest Burro and tried to find out what he could.

"Tell me, Abuela," said Salvador, "did you know about the earthquake?"

"I have known about many earthquakes," answered the Oldest Burro, "but so long as they do not hurt me, I am not troubled by them."

"George the Goat, told me," said Salvador, "that the hacienda was destroyed, and all the human people and all the animal people were killed."

"And yet last night you slept in the shadow of the hacienda and listened to the music of the guitars," she reminded him. "Perhaps George is envious." The Oldest Burro paused to snatch a mouthful of grass. "The grass is very sweet along the sunny road," she said.

Salvador thought that was not a very good answer and he was still a little troubled.

Then one day as they walked down the long sunny road to town, they saw six young soldiers sitting beside the road, smoking cigarettes. Miguel spoke to the soldiers, and sat down and smoked with them for a while. Salvador and all the other burros rested in the shade and ate the sweet grass that grew along the path, being very careful not to eat the lovely red and yellow flowers that grew above the grass. And Salvador was suddenly happy again.

But when they arrived in the town, there was George! And George seemed very much excited. He rushed up to Salvador as soon as Miguel had taken the load of wood off the burro's back, and shouted as loud as a goat can shout: "Did you know that there are soldiers all along the long sunny road to the hacienda?"

"Yes, I knew that," said Salvador. He was quite pleased

with himself that at last he knew the thing George was telling him. He intended to say that they were very pleasant soldiers, but the goat was talking so fast he could not get it said.

"And do you know what they are doing?" asked George.

"Yes," said Salvador. "They are smoking cigarettes."

But George seemed not to hear him, and went right on shouting: "Well, they are shooting all the human people, and even some of the burros and goats. But at any rate there is no one left to feed the burros, and all the animal people that are not killed and eaten will starve to death."

"That is really strange," said Salvador. And now he was very much troubled. "Miguel talked with the soldiers when we came down the long sunny road, and they seemed such pleasant young soldiers. There did not seem to be anyone dead, and certainly they were not shooting anyone when we saw them."

"That is the way it is, though," said George. "They are killing all the human people and all the animal people, and burning all the houses. Everyone in the town knows it. It is only because you are so foolish that you do not see what is happening under your nose."

"Perhaps that is true," said Salvador sadly. "There was the matter of the earthquake. I looked very carefully and I never did see any sign of it. I should never have known about it at all if you had not told me."

Then Miguel came back and told the burros it was time to go home, and they all walked out again along the sunny road. Salvador decided he must talk to the Oldest Burro about this thing that had happened.

"Oh, Abuela!" he said. "Did you know that the soldiers had killed all the human people and many of the animal people on the hacienda?"

"Please do not talk to me," answered the Oldest Burro, who was very wise. "I am tired, and the sun is warm and pleasant, and I want to think about the brook of cool water, and the corn I shall get when we get home to the hacienda. Don't bother me with your foolish questions."

Salvador had a great respect for the Oldest Burro and did not want to be impertinent. So he dared not talk to her any more.

When they arrived at the hacienda everything was just the same as ever. The sun was going down behind the trees, throwing pretty shadows on the white walls of the adobe house. The flowers were tucking their blossoms away for the night, and the birds were twittering in the trees.

All the burros went to the brook and drank the cool water. Then Miguel gave them their corn and sacate. When they had eaten it they lay down in the moonlight and listened to the music of the guitars and to the people singing beautiful songs up by the house.

But Salvador was still troubled. He could not sleep, and kept thinking how foolish he was not to have seen any of the terrible things that had happened at the hacienda. He was very sad because of these things. But he was even sadder because he knew nothing about them. So he decided to run away.

He got up and started running toward the mountain. As he ran he thought how sad it was that all these people were killed, first by the earthquake, and then by the soldiers, and still they knew nothing about it. Then he remembered that George told him no one had been happy there, in the first place. And he was sadder than ever.

Because he was so sad he could not run very fast. After a while he heard someone coming behind him, and suddenly, there was the Oldest Burro, who was very wise, running beside him.

"Why are you running away, Foolish One?" asked the Oldest Burro. "You must turn around now and come home and sleep in the moonlight, because tomorrow we must carry the loads to town."

"I am running away because of all the terrible things that have happened at the hacienda," said Salvador.

But because the Oldest Burro was much older than he, and very wise, Salvador had to obey her. So he turned around and walked beside her, back toward the hacienda.

"And what has happened at the hacienda?" asked the Oldest Burro.

"First of all," answered Salvador, "they say we are all unhappy on the hacienda. And I knew nothing about it. Then came the earthquake and killed everyone. And I knew nothing about that. Then the soldiers came and killed everyone all over again. And I knew nothing about that, either. None of these things did I know until George the Goat, told me about them."

The Oldest Burro snorted and kicked up a little whirl of dust.

"And what did *you* think, Foolish One?" she said. "Did you think you were unhappy on the hacienda? Did you see the earthquake destroy everyone? Did you see the soldiers killing everyone?"

"I thought I was very happy on the hacienda," said Salvador miserably. "And I saw nothing of the earthquake, and the only soldiers I saw were very pleasant young men. But that is probably because I am foolish and cannot see the things that are happening under my nose. That is what George the Goat tells me."

And the Oldest Burro, who was very wise, snorted again —very loudly this time—and kicked up two whirls of dust.

"And this goat who thinks he knows so much!" she said. "This George! He lives in the town and has never seen the hacienda. But we live there. Do you not think then, that we who live there should know more of what happens on the hacienda than the goat, who has never even seen it?"

"I never thought of that!" said Salvador. "You are indeed, very wise, Abuela!"

And he began to run. He ran straight back to the hacienda, and there was everything, just as it had always been. The moonlight was shining on the white walls of the adobe house, and the burros were all sleeping in the moonlight, and up by the house the guitars were playing, and the people were singing beautiful songs.

Salvador looked and looked and felt very happy. Then

suddenly he lifted his head and laughed his long, loud, funny laugh, thinking of how he was going to laugh at George the Goat the next day when he saw him in the town.

For now he saw that it was the burros who lived on the hacienda who knew what happened there. And after all, it was George the Goat, who was the Foolish One.

Salvador and the Coyote

SALVADOR, the little burro, loved living on the hacienda, but then of course, that was the only life he knew. There were many other burros living there, too. At night they all lay out under the stars and slept. If it rained in the night they went into the big shed and slept on the crisp, dry straw, and were very comfortable.

Every morning Miguel came and fed them and put packs

on their backs, and then they all set out on the long sunny road to the town. Salvador loved those trips to town, even if the load on his back was heavy. For he was proud of being so strong, and of knowing just exactly the right place to put his tiny feet so that he could walk fast and not stumble. And he always tried to walk faster than the other burros. In the evening they came home to the hacienda and Miguel gave them corn and sacate. Then all the burros rested in the quiet evening and listened to the human people singing and playing guitars up at the big house.

On Sundays the human people went to church, and the animal people had no work to do all day. So on that day all the burros went for a long walk across the meadow and up the mountainside.

Now Salvador was a timid little burro and considered himself rather stupid. So he always managed to stay in sight of the Oldest Burro, who was very wise. But one Sunday he got so excited over the fresh new grass he found on the mountain meadow that he forgot to watch the other burros. He kept stepping along, nibbling the grass, never once lifting his head. And his stomach was getting fuller and fuller. All of a sudden the green grass ended, and there was a brook flowing along right under his nose.

Salvador was surprised, but the water looked so good that he stuck his nose in and drank. Then he lifted his head, sighed with contentment and looked around him. There was not another burro in sight. But Salvador was not completely alone, for someone laughed quite near him—not a burro laugh.

Salvador pointed his long ears toward the sound and then looked in that direction. There on the other side of the brook sat an animal of a strange reddish color. It looked somewhat like a dog. But Salvador knew instantly that it was *not* a dog, although how he knew it he could not possibly say.

"Hello," said the strange animal. "You must be very hungry. You have been eating like a pig."

"Oh, no," said Salvador. "Pigs eat the roots of plants and do it very noisily. I eat only the juicy green tops of the grass. And the Oldest Burro has taught me to do it very neatly."

The strange animal laughed again. "Maybe you are right," he said. "I guess you eat more like a rabbit, only you give it more attention than the rabbits do."

"Thank you," said Salvador.

He was terribly confused by this conversation, but the odd looking animal appeared to be friendly and Salvador was always ready to make friends. So he sat down on his side of the brook and smiled.

"My name is Salvador," he said. "I am a burro and I live at the big hacienda."

"I already know all that," said the stranger. "I am Raul the Coyote, and I am the wisest of all the animal people. You have probably heard of me."

"Oh, yes," said Salvador. "I have heard my friend, George the Goat, speak of you."

"Of course," Raul the Coyote went on, "my cousin, the fox, claims to be the wisest of the animals, but he is simply sly and not at all to be trusted. But I am really wise, for my wisdom was given me by the ancient gods."

"Oh, I am sure of it," said Salvador. "The Oldest Burro is very wise, too. It must be nice to know so much. As for me, I know that I am very stupid."

"You must be stupid," said Raul, "to spend all your life in the same meadow. Have you ever been to the great woods on the other side of the mountain?"

"Oh, no," said Salvador. "That is too far to go on our one free day."

"Then take several days," said Raul reasonably.

"But I can't do that. For all the other days I must carry the loads of corn or wood or sacate to the town for Miguel."

Raul threw up his head and laughed. "You really are stupid. Why do you carry loads for the human people? Let them carry their own loads. They cannot make you work if you run away. Come with me and I will show you the wide world."

Raul made it sound so easy, seeing the wide world. But Salvador was troubled. He did not know why. All he had to do was cross the brook and go along with Raul. But there was something that bothered him.

"But if I go with you," he said, "Miguel will not know where I am. And there will be no one to give me my corn and sacate at night."

"Who wants corn and sacate!" said Raul scornfully. "Come with me and I will teach you how to find proper food in the woods. You can live the wild free life that all animal people should live."

Just then Salvador heard the Oldest Burro calling him, and realized suddenly that the sun was setting. From far down in the meadow came the loud mournful voice of the Oldest Burro.

"Sa-a-a-al-va—do-oh-oh-hr!" she called.

Before the call had ended Salvador whirled and ran as fast as he could, back across the meadow toward home. He tried to call goodbye to Raul, but his feet were flying so fast he had no breath for talking. And as he ran down the meadow he heard Raul laughing.

All that week Salvador thought about Raul and the exciting life of the animal people who lived in the deep woods. Every time he thought about this he got more and more excited, and more and more discontented with life on the hacienda. He wondered what marvelous kind of food there was in the woods that was so much better than corn and sacate. He, himself, did not know of anything better, but of course he was only a stupid little burro.

One day he tried to ask the Oldest Burro about it. "Abuela," he said. (You know that *abuela* is the Spanish word for "grandmother," and that is what Salvador called the Oldest Burro.) "Abuela, what food is better than corn and sacate?"

"Nothing is better than corn and sacate," answered the Oldest Burro.

"But Raul says—" began Salvador.

"How often have I told you not to listen to gossip," said the Oldest Burro. "Now don't bother me with your questions for I am busy thinking about the new grass in the low meadow."

So Salvador could not find out what Raul meant.

Sometimes he forgot about Raul when they were carrying their loads to town, because he was so interested in trying to keep ahead of the other burros on the long sunny road. And sometimes he forgot about him when he was eating the fresh green grass that grew beside the long sunny road, being very careful not to eat the red and yellow flowers that lifted their heads above the grass.

But at night when the burros came home to the hacienda, and all went to drink the cool water from the sparkling brook, Salvador thought about the brook on the other side of the mountain meadow where he had met Raul. And as he thought about that exciting life in the deep woods, he grew more and more unhappy because he lived on a hacienda and carried loads to town over the long sunny road.

The next Sunday Salvador got up very early, while all the other burros were still asleep. He ran across the low meadow and up the mountain to the farthest side of the meadow, until he came to the brook where he had met Raul. But Raul was not there.

Salvador waited and waited and waited. He grew so hungry that he ate some grass. And then he waited again. Soon it got very hot, so he went and stood in the shade of a

tree and waited some more.

At last it was almost sundown, and Salvador began to think about the corn that Miguel would give the other burros in the evening. He felt rather sad because Raul had not come to tell him more about life in the deep woods. And then suddenly, there was Raul sitting beside a bush on the other side of the stream, although Salvador had not heard him coming.

"Hello," said Salvador. "I have been waiting for you all day."

"Hello," said Raul. "Are you still eating corn and sacate and carrying loads for the human people?"

"Yes," answered Salvador. "But I have been thinking that it must be fine to live in the deep woods and always do exactly what you like to do, and never have to work and get tired."

"Yes, it is a fine life," said Raul.

Salvador was troubled because Raul was not laughing today and seemed to be worried about something. Maybe he had changed his mind about showing Salvador how to live in the deep woods. When he thought that, Salvador was very unhappy because now he was quite sure that he wanted to go away and live a wild free life in the deep woods.

Suddenly Raul stood up. "Well, if you want to come with me, come along. I must go now. I don't like this neighborhood."

So Salvador waded across the brook and he and Raul set off through the bushes toward the woods on the mountainside. It was not very easy to walk with Raul because he did not keep to the path, the way most animals do. He crouched and slunk along in the shadow of the bushes and kept telling Salvador to do the same. But Salvador did not know how to crouch down and crawl under bushes, so after a while he just gave up and walked along the path. He had a hard time keeping up with Raul who traveled very fast in spite of crouching. And it was hard to see him now that it was growing dark.

"I am getting very hungry," said Salvador. "Don't you suppose we could find some corn? Or maybe we could just stop and eat some grass?"

"No," said Raul in a worried voice. "We cannot stop until we get to the deep woods. There are hunters out tonight. Don't you get their scent on the wind?"

Now Salvador had no idea what a hunter was. And the only thing he could smell on the wind was the scent of grass and flowers, and pine trees in the distance, and the brook and the wet earth. But Raul was so worried that Salvador began to worry, too, and he trotted faster up the steep path to the deep woods.

At last they were in the deep woods, where the scent of pine was much stronger, and the earth was soft and damp. It was almost morning and Salvador was very, very tired— much more tired than when he carried the loads to town along the long sunny road. He was terribly hungry, too, but he was almost too tired to think about eating. And now at last Raul stopped.

"Well, here we are," said Raul gaily. "Isn't this fine? Nothing here but animal smells. Now we can think about food."

"I am too tired to think about anything right now," answered Salvador. And he lay down on the soft pine needles that covered the ground.

Raul laughed. "Just as you like," he said. "But it is almost morning, and soon it will be too light to hunt properly."

Salvador thought this was very strange, for anyone can see better in daylight than in the dark. But he was too tired to ask Raul what he meant. Besides at that moment Raul disappeared in the bushes. He made no noise. He just disappeared. Salvador was troubled, for he did not like to be left alone in the deep woods. But he was so tired he could not think about it, so he closed his eyes and went sound asleep.

After a while Salvador was awakened by someone clawing at him. And there was Raul. The sun was up, and everything was so beautiful that Salvador was enchanted. The early sunlight crept under the trees and made lovely patterns on the floor of the forest, which was covered with the soft pine needles. Up in the trees the birds were singing, and Salvador could see the delicate orchids opening their petals. Out in the clearing there was rich green grass, and hundreds of little blue flowers lifted up their heads.

"Come on," said Raul. "It is sunup and we must crawl into the den and sleep."

Salvador thought that a very strange idea, because this was just the time to eat grass. And he could not think what "crawl into a den" meant. But because Raul was so wise and Salvador was so stupid, he knew that he must do what Raul said. So he got up and followed him.

As they crept through the bushes Raul suddenly ducked down and disappeared into the ground. Salvador stood still a moment, staring at the hole where Raul had disappeared. Then he got down on his knees and tried to crawl in, too. But he could not even get his head inside.

He sat still a moment, wondering what to do. Then he heard the birds singing and smelled the green grass. So he got up quietly and went out into the clearing and began to eat the grass, being careful not to eat the pretty blue flowers that lifted their heads above the green.

All day long Salvador ate the green grass. And when he got thirsty he drank from a tiny brook of cool, sparkling water.

All this was very pleasant and Salvador knew he should be happy. But he wasn't happy. He felt faintly troubled all day, because something was wrong and he could not think what it was. Then he worried because Raul stayed so long down inside the earth. Salvador wondered if he would ever come out again.

And then just before sundown Raul suddenly appeared. This was another thing that bothered Salvador. He could never hear Raul coming or going. He just appeared or disappeared.

Raul stretched himself and yawned. "Isn't this a fine life?" he said. "Come on now and we will find something to eat."

"I have been eating grass all day," Salvador told him, "and I am pretty full. But of course I could eat a little corn."

"Corn!" said Raul. "Who wants to eat corn! Remember that you are now a wild animal in the deep woods. From this

time on you will eat proper food. You will eat rabbits and
birds, and will never want corn again."

"Rabbits and birds!" Salvador cried. He was so shocked
that for a moment he forgot how wise Raul was. "Whoever
heard of eating rabbits and birds? Why, they are alive!"

Raul threw back his head and laughed. It was a long loud
laugh and ended in a sort of a wail that made the cold chills
run down Salvador's back.

"Of course they are alive," said Raul. "They would not
be fit to eat if we did not catch them fresh. And while I think
of it, I have been meaning to speak to you about your laugh.
Really, that awful noise you make sounds terrible in the deep
woods. You must learn to laugh the way I do."

Salvador was glad enough to get off the subject of eating
rabbits and birds, so he readily agreed to try to learn to laugh
as Raul did. Raul laughed again to show him how. Then Salvador opened his mouth and tried to make the same kind of
noise. He could start off rather like Raul, but he could not
possibly end in a long wail as Raul did. Salvador's laugh always ended in a throaty "haw-w-w-w-he-e-haw-w-w-
hee-e-e!"

After a while Raul got tired of trying to teach him and
said: "Well, come on. We must go find something to eat
now."

So Salvador and Raul trotted off through the bushes to
another part of the woods. Raul was crouching again and
keeping well under the bushes. But Salvador walked along
the path and thought how beautiful the deep woods were

and wondered what it was that troubled him so much. He could not figure out what could be wrong with this life in the woods.

Suddenly right in front of them, two rabbits jumped up and ran. One rabbit ran east and the other ran west. Raul instantly leaped after the rabbit that ran east.

"This one is my breakfast," screamed Raul. "You take the other one."

But his voice came back from a great distance, because Raul and the rabbit were both running so fast that already they were out of sight.

Salvador stood still in amazement and looked at the bushes where Raul and the rabbit had disappeared. The bushes were still swaying a little, and all the birds up in the trees were crying in fright. Then Salvador heard someone sobbing. He looked around, and there sat the other rabbit that had started to run west.

"Hello," said Salvador. "Why are you crying?"

"Oh, my poor Juanito!" wept the rabbit. "The wicked coyote will eat him. I know he will this time."

"That is terrible," said Salvador, and he, too, began to weep. "Why do you live in the deep woods where Raul can get you?"

The rabbit looked at Salvador in surprise. "Why, where else would we live?" she asked. "This is our home. And it is a fine life, except when the coyote gets hungry."

Salvador shook his head. All this was very puzzling. He could not understand anyone liking to live in a place where

ne did not feel safe. Then all at once Salvador knew what it
was that was wrong with the deep woods, and why he had
been troubled ever since he got here. It was because there
were no human people around to take care of him. At night
he could not hear the music of the guitars and the beautiful
songs that the human people sang up at the big house. He
felt very lonely. And when the rabbit began to weep again
Salvador opened his mouth and wept as loudly as he could.

After a while the rabbit dried her tears, ate a leaf, and
looked at Salvador sociably.

"What is your name?" she asked. "I think you are a
stranger in the deep woods."

"My name is Salvador. I am a burro, and I live at the big
hacienda on the other side of the mountain."

"Oh, yes, I know about burros," said the rabbit. "You
carry loads for the human people and cannot live a wild free
life in the deep woods. That is why I was surprised to see
you here."

"Yes," said Salvador. And every minute he was growing
more lonely and more worried than he had ever been before
in his life. "On the hacienda we burros carry loads for the
human people, but on the other hand, we do not have to
worry about the animal people eating us."

"That may be," said the rabbit, "but I cannot imagine
anyone being happy if he does not live in the deep woods. But
there, I am forgetting my manners. I have not introduced
myself. I am Concha Conejo." (You must know that *conejo*
is a Spanish word and means "rabbit." So Concha Conejo's

name in English would be Concha Rabbit.)

"Thank you," said Salvador. "And the other rabbit who ran east is named Juanito, I believe."

"He *was* named Juanito," said Concha Conejo. "But I expect that by now Raul the Coyote has eaten him. He was my husband. And now my baby rabbits are orphans and I shall have to raise them all alone." Concha Conejo again burst into loud weeping.

Salvador was so lonely that he began to wish that Raul would come back. And then he thought of calling him. He opened his mouth and tried to call as the coyote did—a long cry that ended in a wail. But he could not quite do it. It did not sound like a burro's call, and it did not sound like a coyote either because it suddenly ended in a throaty, sobbing sound of "aw-w-w—w-hee-e-aw-w-w-hee!"

Just then Concha Conejo dropped the leaf she had started to eat and sat up, sniffing the air.

"Oh, my precious whiskers!" she murmured. "Here comes Raul back again! I shall have to go, Salvador. Goodbye." And she darted away into the bushes so fast that Salvador could not see her go.

Salvador did not understand how the rabbit knew that Raul was coming. He, himself, had heard nothing, and had smelled nothing in the air, except the pine trees and the flowers and the soft wet earth. But in just a moment, sure enough, there was Raul standing by the bushes. Salvador had not seen him arrive. Raul looked happy and contented.

"Well, well," said Raul. "You must have caught the other rabbit without much running, since you are still in the same place." He looked around him on the ground. "And I don't see a bit of fur. You must have enjoyed your dinner. Now don't you agree with me that rabbits are much better food than corn?"

But Salvador could not say a word. He turned his head away and felt very sick even at the thought of eating Concha Conejo. But he was afraid to tell Raul that he had just talked with her and had never thought of eating her. Because Raul would tell him again that he was stupid.

Raul laughed and lashed his tail, and picked a thorn out of his hind foot. Then he shook himself and looked at Salvador.

"Well, let us go down to the lower ground and see if we can find a quail for dessert," he said. "I am really quite full, but one can always eat a tasty quail."

Salvador got up without a word and walked after Raul. But he was too sad to talk. He kept thinking about Juanito Conejo and about Concha and her orphaned baby rabbits. Then he thought about the peace and comfort of the hacienda and the music of the guitars, and the safety of knowing there were human people nearby. And suddenly he felt so sorry for himself that he wanted to weep again.

Raul was in a very good humor, and he laughed and told jokes as they walked along. Then he said, "Now, Salvador, aren't you glad you came away to live in the deep woods? Think of the other burros carrying loads to town. And here

you are in the beautiful deep woods, which is the only fine
place to live."

"I suppose," said Salvador, "that *you* have a fine life in the
deep woods. It is very beautiful here, with the bright flowers
and the birds singing all day. But I am quite sure I should not
like to be a rabbit in the deep woods, never knowing when
someone would come along and eat me."

Raul looked at Salvador for a moment and did not say
anything. Just then off in the distance Salvador heard the
faintest echo of a burro call. He was quite sure it was the
Oldest Burro and his heart leaped with joy. But before he
could say a word he saw Raul stiffen, his pointed ears rise, and
the hair on his back stand straight up as he sniffed the air.
Then Raul crouched, ready to spring.

"Run!" shouted Raul. "Run for your life! It's a hunter!
Can't you smell him? And there are dogs, too! I smell them!
Run for your life!"

The coyote leaped away into the bushes so quickly that
he was gone before he finished speaking. Salvador stood and
stared at the bushes where he had disappeared. That was the
trouble with Raul, he thought—you never knew where he
was. One minute he was there, and the next minute he was
gone.

And what did he mean by "Run for your life"? Of course
Salvador could hear the dogs now, but surely no one need be
afraid of dogs. And then all at once Salvador knew that Raul,
the wise one, was afraid! He was afraid of the dogs! Why,
his life was just as bad as the life of the rabbits—always afraid

hat some other animal would come along and kill him!

Salvador was so surprised that he could do nothing but tand still and stare. Then he remembered the word "hunter." f there were dogs, there would be a man with them. That vas it! A hunter was a man! And Raul was afraid of men and logs!

Salvador was very proud of himself for figuring these hings out. Maybe he was not so stupid after all! Then he ealized that the dogs were coming nearer, and that there nust be a man nearby. And there again was the burro call 1e had heard before! Maybe if he followed the sounds he :ould find Miguel and the Oldest Burro. He pointed his long :ars around until he knew from which direction the sound :ame. And then he began to run.

In a moment he met the dogs from the hacienda, but hey did not even stop to say hello to him. They dashed on ıs fast as they could in the direction that Raul had taken.

Salvador lifted his head and called loudly. And sure :nough, from far down the mountainside the Oldest Burro ınswered him. Salvador laid back his ears and ran as fast as ıis legs would carry him. He plunged through the bushes vhich tore at him with their thorns and scratched his skin. 3ut he did not mind that in the least, and kept right on run-ıing.

Presently he saw Miguel plodding up the path with a gun ɔn his shoulder. Behind him came the Oldest Burro, with no oad except a jug of water and Miguel's lunch box. When the Ɔldest Burro looked up and saw him she let out a long satis-

fied call. Then she stepped off the path and began to eat the
sweet green grass of the mountainside.

Salvador leaped over a big rock, stumbled and fell, and
went rolling down the mountainside, landing right at Miguel's
feet. Good burros never stumble, so he was terribly ashamed.
But he was so glad to see Miguel and the Oldest Burro that
he soon forgot his embarrassment.

The next thing Salvador knew, Miguel was examining
him to see if he were hurt. He lay still and thought how nice
it was to be taken care of. Then Miguel took a jar from his
lunch box and rubbed salve on Salvador's scratches and
skinned knees.

"My poor little Salvador," said Miguel. "Don't you know
the tigers will get you if you run away into the deep woods?
Come now, my little burro—try to walk. It is a long way back
to the hacienda and it is almost dark."

So Salvador struggled to his feet and sighed a great sigh.
All this time the Oldest Burro had not said a word. She had
given her attention to eating grass while Miguel was rubbing
salve on Salvador. But now she lifted her head and stepped
onto the path, and she and Salvador walked along side by
side. Behind them came Miguel, and he was singing a song
in his soft young voice. Far away on the mountainside they
could hear the dogs coming back.

Salvador knew he had a long walk ahead of him to the
hacienda, but he was so happy to be with Miguel and the
Oldest Burro that he wanted to sing. He began to think
about the hacienda and the human people who sang songs

and played their guitars. And he thought it was certainly the nicest place in the world to live.

"Where have you been?" asked the Oldest Burro. "And what happened to you?"

"Well, it is a long story," said Salvador.

He felt very important now, because he had been on an adventure and the Oldest Burro was actually asking him to talk about it. Usually he had a hard time getting the Oldest Burro to listen to him. So Salvador told her the whole story, and the Oldest Burro listened, grunting now and then. And she did not interrupt him a single time.

As Salvador talked he remembered all over again how sad and frightened he had been in the deep woods. He remembered, too, how smart he had been to figure out what was wrong with life in the deep woods.

"You know, Abuela," he said. "I realize now that I am not foolish, because I know what is wrong with life in the deep woods. It is Raul the Coyote and Concha Conejo who are foolish, because they think they have a fine life. They do not know that life on the hacienda is much better. So I am wise, am I not, Abuela?"

"No," said the Oldest Burro. "Raul the Coyote and Concha Conejo are wise, because they know they belong in the deep woods. They would never try to live on the hacienda. But you are foolish because, although you were born a burro and are meant to live on the hacienda, you thought you could live the life of the wild animals in the deep woods. No one can be happy in this world until he learns to do the things he was born to do, and lets others live the life they were born for. I hope you will never be so foolish again."

The Oldest Burro kicked up a little whirl of dust and trotted off down the road. Salvador was not sure just what she meant by that speech, but he knew that she was very wise. Then he saw the lights of the hacienda across the meadow, and he kicked up two whirls of dust and trotted after the Oldest Burro. As he trotted he opened his mouth and let out a long happy laugh. It was frankly a burro laugh, and not an effort to sound like some other animal. Salvador thought it was the most satisfactory kind of laugh in the world.

The Foolishness of Cochinito

SALVADOR loved the cool brook and the shade of the big trees and the sound the human people made singing and playing their guitars up in the big adobe house. He even loved the walks to town along the long sunny road, in spite of the load on his back. In fact Salvador loved just about everything and everybody. He was always making new friends, which very often got him into trouble.

One day all the burros went to town with Miguel, the

boy who took care of them. They carried heavy loads of corn on their backs. It was such a hot day that when they got home in the evening, Salvador was very tired. After Miguel had taken off their pack saddles the burros went down to the brook to drink the cool sparkling water.

Beside the path to the brook was an old stone wall that went right down into the edge of the water. The wall made one side of an old corral, but for a long time now no animal had lived in the pen there. As he walked down the path Salvador did not notice anything unusual about the old stone-walled pen, because he was too tired. But when he had finished drinking he heard a strange voice on the other side of the wall.

Salvador wondered who it was. He knew it was not one of the burros, because that was not a burro voice. And because he was a very curious little burro, he went and looked over the stone wall. There, in a mud puddle near the edge of the brook, lay a little black and white pig. Salvador knew about pigs, for a huge family of them was living in the sties on the other side of the meadow. But he had never seen any of them so near the house.

"Hello," said Salvador. "What are you doing here, lying in that filthy mud puddle?"

The little black and white pig grunted amiably.

"Your question is rather stupid," he said. "First you ask me what I am doing, and then you tell me yourself that I am lying in a mud puddle."

"Excuse me," said Salvador. "Of course I can see that you

are lying in the mud, but I don't understand why. For although I am rather stupid, even I can see that you are getting yourself filthy dirty."

"Oh," said the little pig, "that is different. I am lying in the mud because it is cool and pleasant. I like it. And I always do exactly what I like and never anything that I don't like."

"But you are getting dirty," Salvador persisted.

"Of course I am," said the little black and white pig. "But I like that, too."

Salvador sighed and shook his head. Clearly this was a vulgar creature, and there was no use talking to him about mud. It was better just to be friendly and let people do as they liked.

"My name is Salvador, and I am a burro," he said brightly.

The little pig grunted and turned over in the mud. Salvador tried again.

"What is your name?" he asked.

"Cochinito," said the little pig.

"Cochinito!" said Salvador. "But that isn't any kind of name. Anyone knows you are a cochinito, but it isn't a name. It would be the same as calling me Burrito."

(You must know that *cochinito* is simply the Spanish word for "little pig." So the little black and white pig seemed to have no name, but just "Little Pig.")

"What does it matter," said Cochinito, "what I am called, so long as the human people bring me buckets of corn and rich swill every day, and give me a special pen because I am such a handsome pig?"

"Perhaps it doesn't matter so much to a pig," said Salvador. "Of course, all we burros have special names."

"Oh, yes," said Cochinito. "You all have names, and you all work hard every day. I hear Miguel shouting at you in the morning when he starts you off with your loads, and I hear him shouting at you when he brings you home at night. No one ever shouts at me. I have nothing to do all day long but eat and lie in the shade and grub for roots and roll in the mud. Since no one ever shouts at me, I do not need a name."

"I had not thought of that," said Salvador.

Just then he heard Miguel shouting at him, so he turned and trotted up the path. He heard the little pig laughing and saying, "Didn't I tell you?"

But Salvador was glad to hear Miguel shout, for he was calling him to eat his corn and sacate.

The next day when the burros were carrying their loads to town, Salvador kept thinking about Cochinito. Usually Salvador tried to show how strong he was by walking quickly with his load, and it was fun to try to keep in front of the other burros. But today it was very hot and the load seemed unusually heavy. Salvador kept thinking of Cochinito lying in the shade beside the cool brook.

The Oldest Burro paused to snatch a mouthful of the tender grass that grew beside the long sunny road. Salvador paused, too, and looked at the green grass and the red and yellow flowers that showed their heads above the grass. Then he thought of the buckets of corn and rich swill that the human people carried to Cochinito every day. It didn't seem

quite fair. He turned away from the green grass and walked on down the long sunny road.

The more Salvador thought about it, the more unfair it seemed that he should have to work every day, while Cochinito did nothing but lie in the pen behind the stone wall, and eat and roll in the mud. For several days he would not stop to talk to Cochinito, because he felt ashamed that the human people did not prize him as much as they did the little black and white pig.

Every evening when he walked down the path to the brook, he saw Cochinito wallowing in the mud, or munching corn, or grubbing for roots. Cochinito always called to him amiably, and Salvador always replied to him pleasantly. But he did not want to stop to talk.

One evening Cochinito was waiting beside the stone wall, and as Salvador came along the path to the brook the little pig called him.

"Hello, Salvador," said Cochinito. "I've been thinking about you since our visit the other evening, and there is something I want to talk to you about."

"That is very nice of you," said Salvador. "If you will wait until I get a drink of water, I will stop and talk again."

"Better still," said Cochinito, "come back when you have had your supper. Then no one will be shouting at you, and we can talk in peace."

Salvador thought it was not very kind of Cochinito to remind him that he had to work and be shouted at. But after he had eaten his corn and sacate, he went along the path to the brook and stopped beside the old stone wall. Cochinito was waiting for him.

"You know, Salvador," said Cochinito, "I enjoyed our visit the other evening very much. And I must admit that I am sometimes a bit lonesome in my beautiful pen alone, so I have been wondering if you would come and live with me."

"Oh, I couldn't do that," said Salvador. "In the first place I don't like rolling in the mud, and I don't know how to grub for roots. And besides I have to work. It is a great responsibility, carrying loads over the long sunny road."

"Bosh!" said Cochinito. "Don't pretend you like to work. Nobody likes to work."

"Well," said Salvador doubtfully, "I thought I liked to work, but since you tell me it is so nice to do nothing I am not quite sure. But whether I like it or not, Miguel expects me to carry loads to town."

"It is all a matter of habit," said Cochinito. "We pigs have never got into the habit of working, so no one expects us to do anything but lie around and enjoy ourselves. You burros started off wrong. You let the human people find out that you can carry loads, so of course, they make you work."

Salvador was troubled. Cochinito must be right but it was very puzzling. And Salvador could think of nothing to do about it.

"I suppose you are right," he said. "I am very stupid, so I never knew why we have to work while you have nothing to do all day. But since the human people know that I can carry loads, I don't see what I can do about it now."

"Stupid!" said Cochinito. "That is easy. You have only to get out of the habit. Come live with me and pretend you are a pig."

"I had not thought of that," said Salvador.

He jumped over the stone wall into Cochinito's pen.

"What shall I do to start being a pig?" asked Salvador.

"It is time to go to bed now," said Cochinito. "I have a lovely shed in the corner behind the big shade trees. Come along."

Salvador did not like Cochinito's shed. In the first place, it was too low and he bumped his head on the roof. And in the second place, Cochinito was so dirty that Salvador did not like to lie in the straw with him. So he slept outside on the grass. It was not so smooth as the grass beside the burro sheds, for Cochinito had been grubbing for roots and there were hard little ridges everywhere. Also he could scarcely hear the human people singing and playing their guitars up at the big adobe house. And although he hated to admit it, he missed the other burros.

The next morning Salvador woke up early. He was very much excited, thinking that today he was going to be a pig and stay at home and play, instead of carrying a load to town.

He heard Miguel calling him and from force of habit and because he wanted his breakfast, he opened his mouth to bray and started toward the stone fence. Then he remembered that Miguel always put on their loads as soon as the burros finished eating. He stopped. Better just to fill up on grass today. So he ran and hid himself in the bushes beside the brook.

He stayed there a long time, and after a while he could hear Miguel shouting at the other burros as they set out for town. He had not seen Cochinito since he ran to hide. But now the little black and white pig came down to the brook and flopped down in his mud puddle.

"Well," said Cochinito, "you see how easy it is? The other burros have gone to town, and here you are with nothing to do all day but lie in the mud and eat."

"I don't think I want to lie in the mud," said Salvador uncertainly. "And as for eating, the grass here does not compare with that in the meadow. And I must admit that I rather missed my corn this morning."

"I expect you did," agreed Cochinito. "I had a fine breakfast—a pail of delicious swill and a measure of corn. Of course, the human people do not know you are here yet, so they did not bring you any. But as soon as they are convinced you are a pig, they probably will. You'd better come lie in the mud and act like a pig."

Salvador did not like lying in the mud, but Cochinito assured him he would soon get used to it, and then he would see how pleasant it was. As for digging roots, Salvador could not do that at all. Cochinito put his long tough nose into the earth and turned over the sod with the greatest enjoyment. But when Salvador tried it he only hurt his soft nose, and the sod remained as firm as ever. Just the same, it was very pleasant pretending to be a pig, for he could nibble the green grass and think how hot it was on the long sunny road, and how cool it was here by the brook.

At midday the Old Master and the Young Master came down to the pen. They leaned on the old stone wall and looked into the pen. Cochinito ran to his trough to see if they had brought him any food. Then he lay down on the ground and rolled and grunted to show them how fat and beautiful he was.

"He is a very handsome pig," said the Old Master. "See how fat and sleek he is getting!"

"Yes," said the Young Master. "He will be in fine condition for my sister's wedding next week."

Salvador trotted up and sat down beside Cochinito and tried his best to look like a pig.

"Did you hear that?" said Cochinito. "I am to go to the wedding of the Young Mistress next week!"

Salvador had heard and he was very envious. He lay down on the ground beside Cochinito and tried to grunt as the little pig did, so the masters would see him and invite him to the wedding too.

"What is that burro doing in this pen?" said the Young Master. "I thought Miguel was using all the burros to carry corn."

"Who knows?" said the Old Master. "Probably Miguel gave him a day to rest and he has jumped in here for company."

But not a word did they say about inviting Salvador to

the wedding. He looked at Cochinito and spread his ears inquiringly.

"It is all a matter of habit," said Cochinito complacently. "You have not been a pig long enough yet to look like one. In any case you cannot hope to go to the wedding, for only a very handsome pig can be so honored."

"Yes, indeed," the Old Master was saying, "there is nothing like a fat young pig to grace a wedding banquet. We must tell Pepe to give him an extra measure of corn tonight."

The two masters walked away, and Cochinito got up and waddled proudly back to his mud puddle. Salvador followed him with drooping ears.

"I have never been to a wedding," said Salvador.

"Neither have I," said Cochinito. "But I have heard that they are very important occasions."

"Yes," said Salvador. "I have heard that the human people consider weddings even more important than the animal people do."

"And I," said Cochinito, "am probably the only animal person on the hacienda who will be invited to the wedding."

"At least," said Salvador, "there is to be an extra measure of corn, so I shall eat tonight."

"Don't be foolish," grunted Cochinito sharply. "That extra measure of corn is for me. I will share my pen with you and teach you how to dig roots, but you cannot expect me to share my food with you."

Salvador was bewildered and a little troubled.

"But how can I get fat and learn to be a pig," he said, "if you do not let me share your food?"

Cochinito stopped and stared at him with his little black eyes.

"Now that I think about it," said Cochinito, "I don't believe you will ever make a very good pig. Even if you learn to dig roots and roll in the mud, you will never be as fine a pig as I am. I don't know what I was thinking of to invite you into my pen."

"But I *can* eat corn and get fat," said Salvador reasonably.

"Don't be silly!" snapped Cochinito. "Even the other pigs on the hacienda are not permitted to share my pen, and no one else is to be invited to the wedding. I am so much more important than you are that I'm surprised I ever bothered with you. You'd better go away now. I want nothing more to do with you."

Cochinito turned his curly tail on Salvador and waddled away to lie in the shade. Salvador was troubled and unhappy. He jumped over the old stone wall and went to graze in the meadow, while he waited for the other burros to come home.

In the evening when the other burros came back along the long sunny trail, Salvador called to them and ran out to meet them. But Miguel scolded him because he was covered with mud, and all the other burros turned their heads away and would not speak to him. All except the Oldest Burro. The Oldest Burro looked at him with her wise old eyes and knew he had been up to mischief.

"Where did you go last night?" she asked. "And why did you not come to carry your load this morning when Miguel called you?"

"Well," said Salvador, "I thought I would stop working. I thought I would get out of the habit of carrying loads to town. It is very simple. I don't see why everyone is angry with me about it."

"Don't you?" said the Oldest Burro severely. "Well, the rest of us had to carry your load in addition to our own. When one person refuses to work, someone else must do his work for him. None of us like that. You'd better be ready to carry your own load tomorrow."

Salvador went with the other burros to drink at the brook. Then he went with them and had his corn and sacate. But still no one spoke to him. He was troubled and unhappy, for he did not understand why everyone was angry with him, while no one thought of being angry with Cochinito for not working. So when all the burros lay down in the moonlight to sleep, Salvador went over and lay beside the Oldest Burro, hoping to find the answers to the things that were puzzling him.

"Abuela," said Salvador softly. (You remember that *abuela* is the Spanish for "grandmother," and is what Salvador called the Oldest Burro.) "Abuela, why is it that we burros must always work, while the black and white pig has nothing to do all day but lie in the mud and eat, and no one is angry with him for it?"

"Ah, the poor little cochinito!" said the Oldest Burro.

"But why?" persisted Salvador. "Why does Cochinito have so much better life than we do?"

"Be still, Foolish One!" said the Oldest Burro. "We have a much better life than any pig. Ah, the poor little cochinito!"

Salvador did not consider that a very good answer. But the Oldest Burro shut her eyes and went to sleep and Salvador was afraid to talk to her any more.

After that every day Salvador carried his load to town. Every evening he walked with the other burros along the path beside the old stone wall, down to the brook. And every evening he looked over the stone wall at Cochinito, but Cochinito was far too proud to speak to him now. Every day Cochinito grew fatter and lazier and prouder. And every day Salvador was more and more troubled because the black and white pig did nothing at all, and yet was to be invited to the wedding, while he worked every day and was not to be invited.

At last the day came for the wedding of the Young Mistress. That morning very early all the burros went down to the brook to drink the cool water. Salvador looked over the stone wall and saw Pepe scrubbing Cochinito in the brook on the other side of the wall. As they walked back up the path he saw Pepe lead Cochinito away to the unknown regions behind the stables. Salvador was very envious, for he was sure now that Cochinito was going to the wedding of the Young Mistress.

That morning the burros did not go to town along the long sunny road. When Miguel had put on their pack saddles he turned the Oldest Burro's head toward the mountainside.

"There will be no trip to town today, my burritos!" said Miguel gaily. "Today the Young Mistress is to be married, and we must go to the mountainside and bring back plenty of wood from the forest to cook the feast for the wedding guests."

All the burros trotted happily away toward the cool green forest—all except Salvador. He hung back and went so slowly that Miguel had to prod him. When they arrived in the midst of the cool green forest the burros ate berries and nibbled the young green leaves, while Miguel gathered the wood for their loads—all except Salvador. He stood sadly alone, thinking about the glory of Cochinito waddling among the guests at the wedding.

At last the Oldest Burro came and stood beside him.

"What is the matter, my little Salvador?" said the Oldest Burro. "Are you unhappy because the Young Mistress will be going away from the hacienda with her new husband?"

"Oh, no," said Salvador. "We rarely see the Young Mistress. So long as Miguel stays with us I don't care who leaves the hacienda."

"Then why are you sad?" said the Oldest Burro. "Are you grieving for the poor little cochinito?"

"Why should I grieve for Cochinito?" said Salvador. "I am only wondering why it is that he does no work at all. No one expects him to do anything but wallow in the mud and eat all day, while we burros must work for our corn and sacate. Even today, the wedding day of the Young Mistress, we must carry wood from the forest."

"Foolish One!" said the Oldest Burro. "Have you not learned that everyone in this world must be useful? The wild animals in the forest must work to find their food and to escape the dangers that surround them. We who live on the hacienda must work to be worth our care. If the human people feed the pigs and expect no work of them, it is because they will make use of them in another way."

"And yet," said Salvador, "Cochinito has done nothing all his life but eat and grow fat. But he is the only one of the animal people who is going to the wedding."

"Most Foolish One!" said the Oldest Burro, and she stamped her feet and sent up a whirl of dust. "Do you not know that the cochinito's place at the wedding banquet is on the table? This wood you will carry back to the hacienda will be used to roast him in the oven for the wedding guests to eat. And you, foolish, lazy, little burro, will still be alive to carry your loads to town along the long sunny road."

Salvador opened his eyes and stared at her. So that was it!

"Abuela mia!" said Salvador. "You are indeed wise! My work is only to carry loads, but Cochinito's work was to grow flesh on his bones for the human people to eat. Truly, I am a very stupid little burro!"

Salvador kicked up his heels and sent up two whirls of dust. He ran to Miguel and stood to have the load of wood tied on his back. Then as he trotted down the path to the hacienda, he opened his mouth and gave a long shout of burro laughter, for joy that he was alive in the beautiful sunny world.

The Million-Dollar Somersaults

M O R E than two hundred years ago in far-away Spain lived a little girl named Paz. (*Paz* is the Spanish for "peace"; and anyone named Peace should be a very lovable little girl. But, as a matter of fact, Paz was a very disagreeable little girl, so this was not a good name for her.)

Paz's father and mother had both died when she was a very little girl. They had been poor, so Paz was not only an orphan, but she was a very poor orphan and her rich relatives had to take care of her. She was a proud girl and did not like this at all.

One day a letter came from her uncle who lived in Mexico, saying that since he had no children of his own he wanted Paz to be his little girl and come to live with him. This uncle was a rich nobleman whose title was Marquéz del Valle Salado, and was the most important person in the whole family. Of course Paz was delighted. It would be exciting to make the long journey across the ocean to Mexico. And being a very selfish little girl she thought it would be wonderful to be so rich.

Her relatives sent an old woman named Juana to take care of Paz on the boat and bring her safely to her uncle in Mexico. Juana was a nice old woman who had been a servant in the family for a long time. She loved Paz in spite of the fact that the little girl was often so disagreeable.

When they arrived in Mexico, there was Uncle Mendo to meet them and take them to his beautiful house on one of the finest streets in Mexico City. Uncle Mendo was happy to have a little girl of his own to live with him in the big house. Right away he began to give her beautiful things. He bought her so many dresses that she had to change three times a day in order to wear them all in two months. For each dress he bought her beautiful little shoes and a lace shawl and a fan of lace mounted with gold or silver.

Paz was proud and thought she was going to be very happy, too. But she had no time to be happy, because she was so busy being proud of having so many beautiful things and of living in the big house of the Marquéz. And every day she became more disagreeable because she felt so important. By the time she had lived in Mexico City two weeks she decided she was just as important as a princess.

Now it happened that in the same street lived another little girl just the age of Paz. Her name was Carmen. Carmen's father and mother were friends of Don Mendo, and one day Carmen's mother brought her to call on Paz. Don Mendo was pleased because Paz was going to have a friend to play with. But when old Juana went to call Paz, what do you think happened?

Paz said, "Who is this little girl who comes to see me?"

"Her name is Carmen," said Juana, "and she is a little lady."

"Is she a princess?" asked Paz.

"No," said Juana, "she is not a princess, but she will play with you and be your friend."

Paz lifted her chin and looked very haughty. "Only a princess is important enough to be my friend," she said.

Then Juana became terribly worried and unhappy. "Oh, Paz, that is an awful thing to say," she said. "You'd better come down and be nice to Carmen, or Don Mendo will be angry."

So Paz went downstairs, but she was not nice to Carmen. "How do you do," she said very coldly. Then she went over and stood by the window so the visitors could see her beautiful dress. And she would not talk to Carmen at all. Carmen

was so embarrassed and unhappy that after a short time her mother took her home.

When they had gone Don Mendo said, "Paz, my dear, why were you so rude to Carmen?"

Paz lifted her chin and looked very haughty. "Only a princess is important enough to be my friend," she said.

Uncle Mendo was shocked. "That is naughty, Paz. You must like other people, and you must learn to be courteous or you will never have any friends to play with."

"Play?" said Paz. "It is not dignified to play. Only common children play." And she lifted her beautiful fan, held the skirt of her lovely dress with one hand, and swept from the room. She was much too dignified to run.

The next day a little girl named Marina came to see Paz, and Don Mendo sent Juana to call her.

"Well, who is this little girl who has come today?" said Paz.

"Her name is Marina," said Juana.

"Is she a princess?" asked Paz.

"No, she is not a princess," said Juana. "She is just a nice little girl who will play with you and be a good friend."

Paz lifted her chin and looked very haughty. "Only a princess is important enough to be my friend," she replied.

But Paz went downstairs, because she was afraid that if she did not, Uncle Mendo would be angry and refuse to buy her any more pretty things.

"How do you do," said Paz to Marina very coldly. And again she went over and stood by the window so the light would fall on her pretty dress. She opened her little silver fan and waved it gracefully as she had seen grown ladies do. But she would not talk to Marina. So after a while Marina's mother took her home.

The next day Rosita and her mother came, and the day after that a beautiful little girl named Luz. But it was just the same. Paz wanted only a princess for a friend, and no princess came to see her.

Uncle Mendo was terribly worried by this time, because he knew now that Paz was really a most disagreeable little girl. And because he loved her very much he was unhappy about it. But no matter how much he talked to her, she kept right on being disagreeable.

After a while all the other children who lived in that street and all the grown people too, knew that Paz was terribly disagreeable, and they decided not to go near her any more. What was the use of bothering when they knew now that Paz thought it was undignified to play, and that she was rude to everyone who tried to be nice to her. So the days and the weeks and the months went by and no one at all came to see Paz.

One day Paz stood by the window and looked down into the street where all the children were playing. Actually she was very lonely, but she was too proud to admit it even to herself. She stood by the window and waved her fan as she had seen grown ladies do.

And she laughed and said to Juana: "It is very undignified

to play. I would not think of running in the streets the way common children do."

Old Juana shook her head and looked worried. She knew that Paz was lonely and unhappy, and she knew, too, that Paz never would be happy until she learned to be friendly and kind.

Just then a beautiful carriage came down the street. Paz saw the plumes on the horses' heads and the crest on the carriage, and she knew it was the carriage of the viceroy. She had heard that every day at this time the viceroy's little daughter, Princess Isabella, went for a drive in the carriage. So she was sure this was the princess coming to see her. She walked down the long stairs—she was much too dignified to run—and waited in the big sala to receive the princess.

But no one knocked at the door. The princess was not coming to see Paz. And because she was waiting in the sala, Paz did not see the little princess leave her carriage down in the street, and play with Rosita and Carmen and Marina and Luz and all the other children for a long time before she went back to her father's palace.

After that every day when Juana took Paz for her daily drive in Uncle Mendo's carriage, Paz insisted that two of the footmen go along. And she kept the curtains of the carriage closed, because she thought that was the way a princess rode through the town. All the other children thought it was very funny, because Paz was no more important than they were, but she put on more airs than the real princess herself.

So several years passed, and Paz was growing up, just as Marina and Luz and Carmen and Rosita were growing up. But Paz was lonely and unhappy, and she thought it was because there was no one in all Mexico City important enough to be her friend. She did not know that she was unhappy just because she was so proud and disagreeable.

Don Mendo was unhappy, too, because in all these years he could not think of a way to make Paz see how foolish she was, and how much nicer it would be to have friends. Then he thought that maybe she would be happier if she fell in love with a young man and was married.

So Don Mendo invited all his friends who had sons to come to see him. And one by one he introduced them to Paz —all the handsomest young men in Mexico City.

Now Paz was really a very beautiful girl, but she had thought unkind thoughts for so long, and had always been so selfish, that it showed in her face. And people who looked at her saw only her proud disagreeable face, and did not notice that she was beautiful. So as soon as the young men saw her, they made polite excuses and then went home. And not one of them came back to ask Don Mendo if he might marry Paz.

Then one day Don Mendo died. But before he died he had thought of a way to cure Paz of her terrible pride. He knew that she did not love anything but money, and that being rich was the most important thing in the world to her.

Paz pretended she was very sorry, when Uncle Mendo

died, because she thought that was the proper thing to do. Since Uncle Mendo had been so very good to her, she was sure that he had left her all his money and that she would be very rich. And she thought, too, that she would inherit his title and be a marquesa.

So when the man who had charge of Uncle Mendo's money sent for her to tell her about his will, she put on a beautiful black dress and a black lace shawl, and carrying a lovely ebony fan went down to talk to him.

"Paz," said the man, "your uncle has left you all his money, but—"

"Of course," said Paz, "I was sure he would. My uncle loved me very much."

"But," said the man, "there is one condition. We must invite the whole town to gather in the big plaza as for a fiesta. Then you must dress up in your prettiest dress and drive through the streets in an open carriage so that everyone can see you. And when you come to the big plaza you must get out of the carriage and, on a little platform before all the people, you must turn three somersaults. If you do not do this all your uncle's money will be given to the Church, and you will be very poor."

Paz was so angry she could not think of a single word to say. If she had not been so dignified she would have stamped her feet and screamed. But in all her life Paz had never done anything that was not dignified. And now Uncle Mendo, the only person in the world except old Juana, who had ever loved her, had fixed it so she must do such a terribly undig-

nified thing that everyone in the city would laugh at her.
Paz was so angry she wanted to cry. But of course she didn't
cry, because crying was not dignified.

At first Paz said she would not do it. Then she thought
about how terrible it would be to be poor again. Why, she
would not even have enough money to go back to Spain
where her other relatives might take care of her! She would
have to find work, and perhaps be somebody's servant! Paz
thought that would be even worse than turning somersaults!
No matter how embarrassing it was she would have to turn
those somersaults in the plaza!

So the word was sent through the city that on a certain
day everyone was to gather in the big plaza for a surprise.
Then Paz went upstairs and put on her prettiest dress, and
went down and got into the carriage. She had the top put
down, so everyone could see her as she drove through the
streets. Her pretty little face was white and angry. But she
had always looked so disagreeable that no one noticed much
difference in her.

Then she arrived in the big plaza. There were all the
people waiting. And right near the little platform were all
the girls and boys who had tried to be friends with her when
she first came from Spain. Suddenly she remembered how
rude she had been to them, and that she could not blame them
much if they laughed at her now. And she realized that she
had not a friend in the world except old Juana.

Then Paz thought about all the money that her uncle had
left. So she leaned over and put her head down on the little

platform. Up went her feet in the pretty little shoes. Her full skirt fell over her head and everyone in town saw her little white pantalettes. Over she went, landing flat on her back. She sat up quickly and pulled her skirt down. Her curls were down over her face and her ribbon was gone. And all the people roared with laughter.

Paz jumped to her feet, with her curls every which way, and looked at the people. She was so angry that she forgot all about dignity. She jumped up and down and shook her fists at the people. But she remembered then that she still had to turn two more somersaults.

So down went her head again, and up went her feet in the pretty little shoes, and once more she landed flat on her back. She sat up, with her curls every which way. She felt a little dizzy. She had never cried in her life because she had always been too proud. But now suddenly she wanted to cry and she did.

This time when she stood up she did not stamp her feet. She looked around at the people and they all saw the tears that were in her eyes and running down her pretty flushed cheeks. Only a few people laughed this time, and she saw that Carmen and Rosita and Luz and Marina, who were quite near, did not laugh at all. They had tears in their eyes, too, because they were so sorry for her.

But Paz remembered that she still had one more somersault to turn. So once more she put her head down on the little platform. She was learning how to do a proper somersault by now, and this time her feet went over so much faster that her white pantalettes scarcely showed at all. She landed flat on her back, and sat up with her curls every which way.

She sat there and listened for the laughter, but she did not hear any. Then suddenly she thought how very funny she must look, and before she knew it she began to laugh. She laughed and laughed and laughed. Then old Juana climbed up on the platform, and took her hands and pulled her to her feet. But Paz was still laughing. She looked around at the people. They were smiling at her—friendly smiles. Then they all began to laugh, too. But it was quite different now. They were not laughing *at* her, they were laughing *with* her.

And all of a sudden Paz understood that laughing made everything easier; and she realized how much fun she had missed all her life by being so proud and disagreeable. She looked down at Carmen and Rosita and Luz and Marina, who had lived in the same street with her for years and who had tried long ago to be her friends. Then she smiled at them.

"You know," said Paz, "I think it might be fun to turn somersaults, if I were turning them because I wanted to and not because I had to, and if I were turning them at home with some friends, instead of in the big plaza."

Marina and Luz and Rosita and Carmen all smiled at her in the friendliest manner.

"Lots of things are fun when you have friends," said Marina.

"Yes," said Carmen. "Let's all go home and see who can turn the best somersaults."

"Let's!" said Paz. "All of you girls come ride in the carriage with me."

So they all went home together and soon became very good friends. And that is how Paz learned how to laugh and to play and to have friends. Every time she felt like being disagreeable, she remembered how embarrassed she had been when she turned three somersaults in the big place. She never forgot it!

No one else ever forgot it either. They even made up a new name for the street where Paz lived. For two hundred years that street has been called the Calle de la Machincuepa (which is Spanish for "The Street of the Somersault").

The city has grown very big now and that street is old and shabby. When you go to Mexico City you might drive through Somersault Street, yourself. Only I hope you never have to turn somersaults in the big plaza.

The Smoking Mountain

IN THE long-ago days when the world was young two kings lived in a land called Anáhuac, which was in the very middle of Mexico. There were other kings in the land, too, but these two kings were special because they hated each other so much.

One of the kings lived on the south side of a tall mountain, and there the sun always shone, the flowers were very large

62

and bright, and the birds sang all day with high sweet voices. This king was short and round and fat, with a jolly face and a big laugh. He had a very long name, but everyone forgot what it was because everyone called him The Jolly King.

On the north side of the mountain lived the other king. Here the north wind made the sunshine thinner, so it was colder, and the flowers were tall and slender, but their perfume was very sweet. This other king was tall and thin, and his face was long and dark. He did not talk much because he was always thinking deep thoughts about how the flowers grew, how to make the corn have more ears, and about the doings of the gods. For in those days the old gods lived on the earth. This king, too, had a very long name, but everyone had forgotten it because everyone called him The-King-with-the-Thin-Thoughtful-Face. But that name, too, was much too long, so after a while they just called him The Thin King.

The Thin King and The Jolly King hated each other. Long ago when the world was even younger they had a quarrel and made their people go to war. They fought for a long time but neither side could win. After a while the people forgot what they were fighting about, so they all went home and began to look after their corn fields again. But the two kings went on hating each other.

Sometimes someone would say to The Thin King: "I think I will go on a journey. They say there are many strange flowers in the land of The Jolly King, so I think I shall go to see them."

Then The Thin King would be very angry, and would

say: "Don't you dare go to the land of The Jolly King! I hate him!"

"But why do you hate him? I never did know."

"I have so much to think about," said The Thin King, "that I cannot remember. But I do remember that I hate him."

And in the land of The Jolly King, the people would sometimes say to The Jolly King: "Now let me see—what was it you and The Thin King quarrelled about?"

And The Jolly King would get angry and his face would get very red, and he would sputter: "Don't talk to me about The Thin King! I hate him! How do I know what we quarrelled about? It is too long ago to remember. But I still remember that I hate him!"

So the two kings kept right on being enemies, and all the wise men in their two countries could not make them understand how foolish it is to hate anyone.

Now it happened that The Jolly King had a little daughter who was more beautiful than all the flowers that grew in his lovely land. He and his Queen had named her Yoloxochitl (which is an Indian name and means "Heart-of-a-Flower"). It was a very good name for her, because Yoloxochitl loved all the flowers and she wandered all day long on the mountainside where the flowers grew and the birds sang.

Yoloxochitl never went to the top of the mountain because it was so high and there were no paths. No flowers grew on the top of the mountain—only great spiny trees and many huge rocks. But on the side of the mountain there was a lovely path that went on and on. Yoloxochitl used to walk along this lovely path, but she could never follow it all the way around the mountain, because she always had to be home in time for dinner.

One day she started out very early and went much farther than she had ever gone before. Imagine her surprise when the path suddenly ended right in the midst of a grove of flowering trees! There had been the path, plain and clean, with flowers on both sides of it, and then it was gone, and there was nothing among the flowering trees but a funny little stone wall that wound around to miss the trees.

Now Yoloxochitl was a bright girl and knew the geography of her country. So she knew that the little stone wall meant this was the end of her father's kingdom, and that really she should turn around and go straight back to the palace.

But just then she heard a voice singing on the other side of the grove of the flowering trees. It was a beautiful voice and it sang a gay song of love. Yoloxochitl thought it was sweeter than all the birds' voices she had ever heard. She knew she would be late for dinner, but she stood still beside the little stone wall and listened. The singer was coming nearer. She could not hear his footsteps, but the song came nearer. Then all of a sudden, there he was on the other side of the little stone wall.

He was a young prince, with a beautiful brown face and great black laughing eyes. He wore a white cloak embroidered in bright colors, and about his neck hung a great jewel to show all the world that he was a royal prince.

Yoloxochitl looked into the prince's eyes, and she heard her own heart singing. She thought: "I must be grown up. I can't be a child any longer, because I am in love."

The young prince was staring at her, too. Now he asked: "Who are you? You look like the heart of a flower."

Yoloxochitl laughed. "That is my name," she said. "My father is the king of this land. Who are you?"

The prince told her he was called Tepetl (which is an Indian word that means "mountain"). He was called Tepetl because he was a prince. Someday he would be the king of his country, and his people expected him to be strong as a mountain so that he could look after them. So it was that Tepetl and Yoloxochitl became friends.

After that, every day they both came to the little stone wall and talked; and every day they grew more in love. One day the prince said that it was time they married, so that when he became the king of his land he would have a queen in his palace. Yoloxochitl thought so, too.

"We will go at once to my father and ask him to prepare a feast for the wedding," she told him.

But Tepetl said: "Oh, no! We must go first and tell my father. For it is the custom for my father to go to your kingdom and ask for you to be my queen."

So Yoloxochitl stepped over the little stone wall, and they walked through the grove of the flowering trees. And there was another path. It was wider and harder than the path on her side of the wall, and the flowers that grew on both sides of the path were tall and slender, but their perfume was very sweet.

They walked for a long time. And in the evening, just in time for dinner, they arrived at a beautiful palace. Tepetl led the little Princess Yoloxochitl straight to his father, the king.

Tepetl said: "Look, Father, I have found a princess whom I want for my queen."

The Thin King stopped thinking about the names of the stars, and looked at Yoloxochitl. Her face was so sweet and smiling that before he knew it The Thin King was actually smiling at her.

"She is a beautiful princess," said The Thin King, "and she should be a good queen for our people."

Tepetl said: "Then you will go at once to The Jolly King and ask him if I may marry her?"

Then The Thin King jumped up and moaned and put his hands to his forehead.

"Oh, this is terrible, terrible!" he cried. "The daughter of The Jolly King! Of course you cannot marry her! Send her out of my kingdom at once!"

Then Tepetl said boldly: "Father, I am going to marry her. If you send her away I shall go, too. Why can't you forget about hating The Jolly King?"

"I do forget it when I am thinking," said The Thin King, "but I still hate him. I won't have his daughter in my palace! Send her away! And if you go with her you can never come back. You will never be the king, and I shall learn to hate you, too."

Tepetl and Yoloxochitl were very sad. But Yoloxochitl said that her father was so jolly she was sure he would forgive them and let them live in his palace. So they started out on the long path again. It was very dark now and Yoloxochitl was afraid. So they stopped at the house of a farmer and asked whether they might sleep there.

The farmer said: "Oh, no, Tepetl. The king has said that you are not to rest in his kingdom so long as the maiden is with you. If I let you stay here I will be in great trouble."

So they had to go on again. They walked and walked, all through the long dark night. At last they came to the little stone wall. They stepped over it and went along the narrow path between the big bright flowers. And in the morning they came to the palace of The Jolly King.

He was just eating his breakfast when they came in, and Yoloxochitl led Tepetl right up to the table.

"Look, Father," said Yoloxochitl, "I have found a prince I want to marry. Then when I am the queen he will be my king."

The Jolly King laughed his big laugh and looked at Tepetl.

"That's splendid," he said. "I have been wishing you would find a prince. He is fine looking and should be a good king. But what about his own kingdom? His people will want him to live there."

"Oh, no," said Yoloxochitl. "His father, The Thin King,

says we cannot live in his kingdom, because he is so foolish that he hates you."

Then The Jolly King jumped up and knocked over the table. And he stamped his feet and shook his fists.

"The Thin King!" he cried. "The son of The Thin King! Of course you cannot marry him! Send him away at once! I hate him because I hate The Thin King!"

"But why, Father?" asked Yoloxochitl. "Why do you hate The Thin King?"

"How do I know why I hate him? It is so long ago that I have forgotten. But I still hate him! Send his son away at once!"

Yoloxochitl was very unhappy for she loved her jolly father very much. But she said bravely: "If you send him away, Father, then I must go, too, because we love each other."

"If you go with him you can never come home again!" said The Jolly King, who was not at all jolly when he was angry.

So Yoloxochitl and Tepetl had to go away from that palace, too. They walked away across the fields where the bright flowers grew. The colors in the dress of Yoloxochitl, and the embroidery on the white cloak of Tepetl were as bright as the flowers. The people looked after them and thought how beautiful they were; and everyone was very sad.

At the very edge of the kingdom of The Jolly King they stopped at the house of an old woman whom Yoloxochitl knew. They asked her if they might rest there and have food to eat, because they were tired and hungry. But the old woman was very frightened and said: "Oh, little Yoloxochitl, you know how much I love you, but now the king says that you are not to rest in his kingdom so long as the young prince is with you. You must go on or you will get me into great trouble."

The Prince and Princess were very tired now, but they had to go on and on. At last they came to the palace of a king that ruled in another kingdom. This king was called The Rich King, because the fields in his land were so rich.

Tepetl and Yoloxochitl knocked at the door, and when the king came, Tepetl said: "We want to live in your country and be your subjects, because our fathers will not let us marry and live in our own kingdoms."

Tepetl took from his neck the great jewel that showed he was a royal prince, and offered it to The Rich King, saying, "I will give you this jewel for a little house and a little land, where we can live and raise a garden."

But when The Rich King saw the jewel he was very frightened. He said: "Oh, you are Tepetl and Yoloxochitl! You must go away at once! If I let you rest in my kingdom The Thin King and The Jolly King will both be angry with me. They will send their armies to make war on me. If the soldiers tramp over the fields and ruin the grain my people will starve! You must go away at once!"

So again Tepetl and Yoloxochitl had to go away. They were very, very tired now, and it seemed there was no place in the world where they could rest. They went to another

of the neighbor kings, and to still another, but it was the same everywhere. All the kings were afraid to let them rest in their countries, because they feared The Thin King and The Jolly King would come to make war on them.

For a year and a day they wandered about the land, hunting a place where they might live and be happy. But although the people loved them and felt sorry for them, they dared not let them stay in their countries. And all because The Thin King and The Jolly King hated each other over a quarrel they had both forgotten long ago.

The Prince and Princess were so tired they could not search for a home any longer. Then one day Tepetl said: "There is only one place left for us. We will go to the very top of the mountain between our two kingdoms. No one lives there, and it does not belong to any king, so it may be that there we can rest."

So they set out to climb the high mountain. There were no paths and the trees were large and spiny, and there were many great rocks and steep cliffs. But at last they reached the top.

They could look down on all the beautiful world. There on the south side of the mountain was the kingdom of The Jolly King. And on the north side of the mountain was the kingdom of The Thin King. In both these kingdoms were bright flowers and flowering trees and fields of corn. But here on the mountain top it was cold and barren. Yoloxochitl shivered.

"My father's kingdom is very beautiful, isn't it?" she said. "You know, Tepetl, I still love my father and our people. I had meant to be a good queen in my country."

"I know," said Tepetl. "I love my father and our people, too. I had hoped that we might rule our kingdoms together. I wanted the people to forget the old quarrel of our fathers and live as one kingdom, all together in peace."

They sat down sadly on the mountain top, and thought about how much unhappiness hatred made in the world. But just then a strange thing happened. They heard a voice behind them.

"Tepetl! Yoloxochitl!" said the voice.

They whirled around to look, and there stood a young god! You remember that all this happened many years ago, when the old gods still lived on the earth. The young god was tall and strong and handsome. His crown was made of pure sunshine, and his cloak was of shining white snow. They were so surprised that neither of them could think of a word to say.

"You see I know all about you," said the god. "I come from the old gods to bring you a gift. For a year and a day the gods have watched you, and we have seen how well you love each other, and how unhappy you have been because there is hatred in the world. So we have decided to give you a gift."

"What is it?" asked Tepetl. "Are you going to make our fathers stop hating each other?"

"No," said the god, "I cannot do that. Men must learn

by themselves not to hate each other. Until they do learn there will be evil in the world. Even the gods cannot change that. Men themselves must do it. This gift of the gods is just for you. From now until the end of time you will have all the kingdoms of this land at your feet. The time will come when the kingdoms will fall, and other nations will rise, but so long as the land shall last, you will be here, together and happy."

"How?" cried Tepetl. "How will you do this thing?"

But the god did not answer, for he was no longer there. Yoloxochitl and Tepetl looked at each other in surprise. They did not know what the god meant, but they felt happy again. It was getting dark now and the wind on the mountain top was very sharp.

"I am cold," said Yoloxochitl, "and I am still afraid of the dark."

"I will build a fire," said Tepetl. "That will light the night and keep you warm."

So he built a fire on the mountain top, and they sat beside it under the cold stars. After a while Yoloxochitl was sleepy. She lay down to sleep, and Tepetl sat beside her and kept the fire going. Then he slept, too, sitting upright beside the fire.

When morning came the prince and the princess were no longer there. In the night the gods had changed them into two great mountain peaks. And the young god had covered them both with his own soft cloak of pure snow. There was Yoloxochitl, lying down as she had been when she went to sleep; and near by was another tall peak that was Tepetl. Even the fire they had built was saved. Its flame and smoke poured out of the top of the tall mountain.

The people in the land saw the two new mountains, but they did not know then that they were Tepetl and Yoloxochitl. In the warm cloak of snow these new mountains stood out white and shining in the morning sunlight, taller now than all the other mountains around them.

The people looked in wonder and gave the two new mountains names. One looked like a great white lady lying asleep, so that one they named Ixtlaccihuatl (which is an Indian name and means "The Sleeping Lady"). The tall mountain near by, with the smoke pouring from it, they named Popocatepetl (which means "The Smoking Mountain").

All this happened thousands of years ago. Since then many things have taken place in Mexico. But The Sleeping Lady and The Smoking Mountain still stand in the middle of Mexico, with all the country at their feet. They still wear their cloak of white snow. Sometimes the fire goes out, but sometimes you can still see it smoking.

If you don't believe me, you may look on a map of Mexico, and you will find the two mountains there—just two mountains now—named Ixtlaccihuatl and Popocatepetl.

Saint Quien Sabe

ONCE upon a time in Spain there was a stonecutter. All day he worked at cutting up great stones and making them into images of Jesus and the Virgin Mary, and of all the saints. He was a very devout man and loved making images of the saints. Sometimes he made Saint Francis and sometimes Saint Anthony. In fact, he knew about almost all the saints that had ever lived, and at some time or other he had made figures of all of them.

One day when he went out to bring in some stone to cut into images, he found two rather small stones lying close together. They were exactly the same size and the same shape, and he thought: "I shall make two saints that will always go together." So he took them to his shop and began to cut the stone.

He could not make up his mind what saints they were to be, but even so he could not stop working on them. Nor could he decide which to finish first. He worked a little on one, then a little on the other, so that they were both changing from stone into figures at the same time. Slowly these two pieces of stone became two very beautiful little saints. But still the stonecutter did not know what saints they were.

At night when he went to bed the stonecutter left them side by side on his workbench. And one night one of the little figures looked at the other and said:

"What is happening to us? Look! We are not just stones any more!"

"Quien sabe?" said the other little figure. (You see, since they were in Spain they were speaking Spanish, and *quien sabe* is Spanish for "who knows".)

"But look at our hands," said the first little figure. "From the way we hold them we seem to be praying. That must mean that we are saints. But what saints are we?"

"Quien sabe? Who knows?" said the other little image.

"But—que pasa?" said the first little saint (which is Spanish for "what is happening"). He was very curious. "I should really like to know what I am to be called."

The second little saint was tired from being worked on all day by the stonecutter, and besides he was a little lazy. So he said, not very pleasantly: "You ask too many questions. Who cares what saints we are? If you want to know what you are to be called—I shall call you Que Pasa, because you are always saying, 'Que Pasa—What Happens!'"

Now the first little saint was annoyed because his friend did not want to answer his questions. So he said, not very pleasantly: "And you—I shall call you Quien Sabe, because that seems to be all you can say—'Quien sabe—Who knows.'"

In spite of this bad beginning, the two little saints were very good friends by the time the stonecutter had finished them and put them up on the shelf in his shop. There they stood, side by side, just the same size and looking very much alike, with their beautiful little faces lifted and their stone hands folded before them as though they were praying.

"What do you suppose is going to happen to us now?" said Que Pasa.

"Who knows?" said Quien Sabe.

Then something did happen to them—something very exciting. One day a Franciscan priest came into the shop. He told the stonecutter that he was going, with many other missionary priests, in a big boat across the ocean to Mexico, and that he wanted to buy some saints to take with him.

Now you understand that all this happened four hundred years ago, when there was no one living in Mexico except the Indians who had always lived there. The priest told the stone-cutter of how Cortéz had gone across the ocean and fought with the Indians and conquered them, so that Mexico now belonged to Spain. The missionary priests were going across the ocean to teach the Indians about God and Jesus and Mary and the Saints, and they wanted to take with them images of all the saints to give to the Indians. So the stonecutter and the priest went around the shop deciding which images should go out to Mexico.

At last they came to the two little figures standing side by side on the shelf. The priest looked at them and frowned. He was puzzled.

"What saints are these?" he said; because they did not look like any special saints, but just like themselves.

The stonecutter still had not decided which saints they were to be, but he was ashamed to say that. So he thought very quickly, and because the priest was a Franciscan, he said: "Well—ahem!—these are both Saint Francis."

The priest still frowned a little. "They do not look especially like Saint Francis," he said. "But they are a good size, and perhaps no one will notice that they do not look much like Saint Francis. I will take them, too."

"What happens now?" said Que Pasa, who was a little worried.

"Quien sabe? Who knows?" whispered Quien Sabe. And because he was Spanish he wanted very much to make a gesture with his hands when he said that. He tried so hard that his little stone hands actually came apart just a wee bit.

The two small figures were packed up and carried to a boat, and started on the long journey across the ocean. Now-

adays when people cross the ocean, they go in very large boats and the trip takes only a few days. But four hundred years ago boats were very small, and had no motors, only sails. So they had to depend on the wind to carry them across the ocean, and sometimes it took many weeks or even many months to get across. So for weeks the little figures lay in the dark hold of the ship. Sometimes it was so quiet they could not be sure they were moving at all. Other times, when there was a storm, the ship tossed about so much that they rolled against each other and got very seasick.

Then little Que Pasa was worried and unhappy, and said: "Pues, que pasa? What is happening now?"

And Quien Sabe, who did not like to talk when he was seasick, answered crossly, "Quien sabe? Who knows?"

But at last they arrived in Mexico. They were taken off the boat and carried through a strange little town. It was very hot, and there were many flowers, and trees with strange fruits. And the people who came to the doors and into the streets to watch them pass, had black hair and beautiful brown bodies. After the little figures had been carried through the town, they waited while the priests made ready for another journey.

You see, four hundred years ago there were no railway trains, and people traveled on foot, or on horses or burros. So at last Quien Sabe and Que Pasa were put on the back of a little burro, and started on the long journey across the mountains.

At first it was very hot. But when they came to the mountains and began to climb higher and higher, it grew colder and colder. The priests who walked beside the burros put blankets around their shoulders. And at night when they camped on the mountains they built big fires to keep warm. But Que Pasa and Quien Sabe had only their long stone robes that the stonecutter had made for them, and they longed for the hot flowering country they had left behind. Then one day they reached the very top of the mountain and began to go down the other side. And now it grew warmer again, and the sun was bright and the flowers bloomed with gay colors.

They came to a large city that lay on islands in the middle of a big lake. It was the most beautiful city they had ever seen! And to this day it is a beautiful city. Nowadays the water is gone from the lake, and the city is on land like other cities, and is called Mexico City. But four hundred years ago, when Quien Sabe and Que Pasa first saw it, it was called by its Indian name, Tenochtitlan. It covered the small islands in the lake; and people went to see each other over narrow stone bridges.

Quien Sabe and Que Pasa would have liked very much to live in Tenochtitlan, although Que Pasa was always thinking how easy it would be to fall into the lake and be lost under the water. But Quien Sabe did not worry. He never worried about anything. He had always been a little bit lazy, and now the warm sun was making him lazier, so that it was too much effort for him to worry.

The two little figures did not stay long in Tenochtitlan.

For now the priests separated and went off to build churches in far-away Indian towns. The images were separated, too, some going with one priest and some with another.

"What happens now?" said Que Pasa. "Do you suppose they are going to separate us—send you to one place and me to another?"

"Who knows?" said Quien Sabe. And then, for almost the first time, he said something else. You have noticed that Quien Sabe was always too lazy to answer Que Pasa's questions. He never said anything except, "Who knows?" But this time he suddenly realized that all his life he had been with Que Pasa, and just to think of being separated from him made him lonesome.

So he said: "Who knows? But I hope they will not separate us. I think I should be very unhappy without you, Que Pasa, even if you do ask too many questions."

Then one day a fat jolly priest came to get some saints to carry away to his town. He looked at the two little figures lying side by side, and because Que Pasa was nearer he picked him up.

"What happens now?" screamed Que Pasa.

"Who knows?" cried Quien Sabe, who did not want to be left behind.

Now you may remember that Quien Sabe was always trying to make a little gesture with his hands when he said, "who knows?" and that he had managed to get them a wee bit apart. Now he grabbed with his little stone hands and managed to catch hold of Que Pasa's robe. So that when the

priest tried to pick up Que Pasa, the two figures clung together.

"Well," said the fat jolly priest, "it looks as though they
both want to go!"

And so he took them both. Once more the small figures
were mounted on a little burro and started off over the mountains. They were very happy because they were still together.
And Que Pasa, for almost the first time, said something that
was not a question.

"You really are a friend," he told Quien Sabe. "For one
who is so lazy you certainly worked hard to get hold of my
robe and be taken along."

But Quien Sabe only yawned. There seemed no point in
talking about it, now that they were on the way and still
together.

So once more, for many days, they rode over the mountains. They came to another beautiful lake with islands in
the middle of it. But they went past it and down the mountain on the other side, where it was warmer and there were
many beautiful flowers.

At last they came to the most beautiful village they had
ever seen. It was quite different from the big city of Tenochtitlan. This town lay in a little nest of hills on the side of the
mountain, and there were several tiny rivers flowing through
it. All the flowers were very big and bright, and the air was
always sweet with their perfume. There were great gardens
of trees with amazing fruits, and all the people were gay and
happy. The name of the village was Uruapan. And to this day

it is called Uruapan and still looks very much as it did four hundred years ago.

As soon as they arrived in Uruapan the fat jolly priest went to work to build a church, and very soon it was finished. It was quite a small church, but it was strong and sturdy and built to last for many years. It stood at one side of the plaza, which was in the very center of the town. Over the wide door there was a niche, just the right size for one small saint. The fat jolly priest came one day and took Quien Sabe and put him up in the niche. But there was no room for Que Pasa beside him.

"Now what happens?" said Que Pasa. "What is to become of me?"

"Who knows?" said Quien Sabe, wriggling comfortably into his niche where the warm sun fell on him. He looked down into the plaza where people were resting in the shade of the big trees, and he yawned. He was sure Que Pasa would not be far away.

But he was. The fat jolly priest had decided they must have a little chapel out at the cemetery, on the side of the mountain just beyond the town. So he built a small chapel, and over the door he made another little niche, just the right size for one small saint. And of course you know what happened.

Poor little Que Pasa, who always wanted to know what was going on, was taken out and put up in the niche on the chapel, so far away that he could not see the plaza nor watch the people in the town. He could look through the tops of the trees and see Quien Sabe in his little niche. But he was so far away that it was necessary to shout very loud to make him hear.

A hundred years passed, and Quien Sabe and Que Pasa still stood in their two little niches, looking at each other through the tree tops. Every morning, as soon as the sun came up, Que Pasa would shout:

"Yoo-hoo! Que pasa allá?" (which is Spanish for "Yoo-hoo! What is happening down there?")

It was so difficult to make Quien Sabe hear him that Que Pasa kept trying to lift his little stone hands to his mouth to make his voice carry farther. And little by little in the hundred years, he raised them almost to his mouth. And every morning, and every noon, and every evening he would shout to Quien Sabe:

"Yoo-hoo! What is happening down there?"

And Quien Sabe would shrug his little stone shoulders, spread his small stone hands a little wider each year, and answer, "Who knows?"

When Quien Sabe and Que Pasa first came to Uruapan and the fat jolly priest put them into their niches, the Indians had asked: "What saints are these?"

And the fat jolly priest had said: "They are both images of Saint Francis."

But the Indians did not know very much about Saint Francis. They had never seen him, but they could see Quien Sabe and Que Pasa, and very soon they grew fond of them.

Of course, you understand that most people could not

hear Quien Sabe and Que Pasa when they talked to each other. The fat jolly priest, for instance, thought they were only stone images of a saint. He never expected to hear them talk, and so of course he never did. But with the Indians it was different. Because they were so fond of Quien Sabe and Que Pasa they often heard them shouting to each other.

After many years someone noticed that Que Pasa's hands were lifted much more than they had been at first, and that Quien Sabe's hands were spread apart in a gesture one naturally makes when he says, "Who knows?" After a few more years someone actually heard what they were saying, but by that time everyone had forgotten they were supposed to be Saint Francis. So after a hundred years all the Indians called them Que Pasa and Quien Sabe. And now the two little figures were happier and felt more at home.

Another hundred years passed and there were new priests who built new churches. But still the old church stood on the plaza and the little chapel stood out by the cemetery. And every morning, and every noon, and every evening Que Pasa would shout to Quien Sabe:

"Yoo-hoo! What is happening down there?"

And Quien Sabe, being much too lazy to tell him what the people were doing in the plaza, would shrug his little stone shoulders and say, "Who knows?"

Then still another hundred years passed and there was a war in Mexico. You see, by this time Mexico had decided that she did not like belonging to Spain, so she made a war and drove the Spaniards back across the ocean. And after that Mexico was an independent country. This war lasted a long time.

One day, while they were still fighting the war, the soldiers of the enemy came to Uruapan and tried to enter the town to burn the houses. But the people of Uruapan fought very fiercely and overcame them. The cemetery, however, was outside the town, and before the soldiers of the enemy rode away, they not only burned what they could of the little chapel, but tore down its stones and smashed them into bits. Poor little Que Pasa, being a part of the chapel, fell into the ruins and was smashed up along with the stones.

From down on the plaza Quien Sabe in his niche watched the chapel fall. But he could not see what happened to Que Pasa. For more than a hundred years now, he has been waiting for Que Pasa to start shouting to him again.

To this day Quien Sabe stands in his little niche in the old church on the plaza. But he no longer says, "Who knows?". Even though he is still called Quien Sabe by the Indians, who love him, he does not say it any more. He only spreads his little stone hands quite wide apart and asks all day:

"Where is my dear little friend?"

And the Indians, who love him, do not like to tell him what happened to Que Pasa. So they look at him, and spread their hands, and say:

"Quien sabe? Who knows?"

The Story of Ticho

TICHO knew that he was beautiful. He was spotted a very
dark bay with a great deal of white, and he had a black mane
and tail. Mateo, the boy who took care of him, rubbed and
polished him every day, so he was always clean and shining.
His tail was long and silky, and his neck was always arched.
His mane was flung up in a great curl which was perfect for

small children to hold onto, to keep from falling. That marvelous curl was always the same, and his legs were always lifted and reaching out to run. For you see, Ticho was a little wooden horse on a merry-go-round.

It was a very large merry-go-round, and there were twenty other little wooden horses on it. It was a happy life for them. Mateo and his father went about from one big city to another, wherever there was a fair, and set up the merry-go-round. Then all afternoon and far into the evening, the children would crowd round to have a ride. When all the little horses had riders the music would begin, and then they would race like mad around the great circle under their tent. And Mateo would go and stand by the calliope and sing the songs it was playing. Ticho loved being a wooden horse on a merry-go-round.

He especially liked it when just before Christmas they went to the big fair in Mexico City that lasted two weeks. All the little horses were in high spirits then and often argued a great deal.

On the very first day of the fair Ticho got into an argument with Mantequilla. Mantequilla was the horse just in front of Ticho on the merry-go-round. He was a beautiful yellow, just the color of butter. In fact that was his name. (For *mantequilla* is a Spanish word that means butter, so the little wooden horse was really named Butter.)

Ticho and Mantequilla (or Butter, if that is easier to say) began arguing about something they had often argued about before.

"Poor Ticho," said Mantequilla. "How unhappy it must make you to have me always just in front of you, where you can see my beautiful white mane and tail and my lovely color. Doesn't it make you sad because you are not beautiful, too?"

Ticho switched his silk tail and snorted. "Many people think I am more beautiful than you. I notice that I usually have a rider before you do."

"And it must make you unhappy," Mantequilla went on serenely, "because I can run faster than you. No matter how fast you run you cannot pass me. I am always just in front of you. I run faster than any horse on the merry-go-round. That is why I am always at the head of the ring."

"You? At the head of the ring?" said Ticho nastily. "Why, Black Bolo is always just in front of you, and Blanco is in front of him, and Duende is in front of Blanco, and all the others in front of them, until it gets clear around to me. That makes me at the head of the ring, and you at the very end."

"Now Ticho, don't be silly!" said Mantequilla, and he twitched his butter-colored ears angrily. "How can you say you are at the head of the ring, when I am always in front of you?"

"And how can you say you are at the head of the ring when Black Bolo is always in front of you, and Blanco is in front of him, and—"

"Don't go over that again," shrieked Mantequilla. And he tried so hard to stamp his feet that the little iron post on which he was balanced began to squeak and cry out. And Mateo came running to see what was the matter.

There was no way to settle their arguments. No one knows whether a spotted pony is more beautiful than a butter-colored pony, or the other way about. Because some people like spotted ponies better, and some like buttered-colored ponies better, and there are even people who don't admire either one very much. And certainly there is no way to decide which little wooden horse on the merry-go-round is at the head of the ring. They both knew that, but they were very stubborn little horses and neither of them would give in.

Mateo put some oil on Mantequilla's iron post. Then he went and opened the gate where the children were waiting with their tickets, to come in and ride.

"You see," said Mantequilla, "I am at the head of the ring, because they stop the merry-go-round so that I am exactly opposite the gate."

"Only your hindquarters are opposite the gate," said Ticho. "My whole front half is exactly opposite the gate. And one's head is more important than one's tail. So I am certainly at the head of the ring."

"It makes no difference which end is opposite the gate. You think hindquarters are not important, but you would look funny without any."

"And you would look very funny without a head and forequarters," said Ticho. His voice was suddenly very mild and pleasant, for just then a pretty little girl with black curls climbed onto his back.

Ticho squeaked companionably, and tossed his head and his curled mane to show her what a good horse he was. Then the music started and Mateo began to sing, and they all began running like mad round and round the circle.

That night a terrible thing happened. It happened very late, after all the people had gone home from the fair. The street lights were burning, up by the big Monument of the Revolution, and there was a nice white moon in the sky. Ticho was dozing on his little iron post when, suddenly, a chilly little wind sprang up and shook the canvas of the tent.

Ticho looked up and saw a whole family of clouds come charging over the mountains far to the east. And right behind them came a huge angry wind that had broken away from a storm on the gulf and come to find out what damage he could do in the mountains.

Before Ticho could wake Mantequilla to tell him about it, the storm was on them. The clouds spilled a little rain, and the great wind picked up the dust and peanut shells and confetti from the ground and flung them on the horses. Then he grabbed the tent and shook it. Mateo and his father came running to make the tent safe. But before they got there, down it came, right on top of all the little horses. And a big pole fell on Ticho.

The huge wind and the family of mean, black clouds laughed, and gave the confetti and peanut shells a final whirl as they ran away. It was morning before the tent was set up again and all the little horses restored to their places.

Ticho was still on his little iron post. But the falling tent pole had scraped the paint from one of his shoulders, leaving only the bare white wood. And both his slender curved front legs were broken off completely! Mantequilla's paint was scraped off in a great gash down over his hip and hind leg, and his beautiful tail was gone.

They were both silent while Mateo doctored them. He brought some long nails and nailed Ticho's legs on again, but the broken places showed and both legs sagged a little. He found the remains of Mantequilla's lovely tail and nailed it on, too. Then he got some white paint and smeared it on Ticho's scraped shoulder. Ticho knew it did not look just right. Then Mateo put the white paint on Mantequilla's scraped hip, too, because he did not have any yellow paint.

"Well," Ticho sighed when Mateo had finished, "I guess we are neither one very beautiful now, Mantequilla. So there's no need to argue about it any more."

"I admit that," said Mantequilla. "The idea of putting white paint on a butter-colored horse! But I'm still at the head of the ring. Thank goodness, an injured tail does not interfere with my running. But you—surely now you will stop saying you are at the head of the ring. With those broken legs it will be a wonder if you can run at all."

Ticho looked down at his legs and remembered the graceful curve they had had yesterday. He thought that Mantequilla was probably quite right, but he was still too stubborn to admit it.

"We'll see," said Ticho softly. "I think I can run fast enough to stay at the head of the ring, even with broken legs."

But as that day went on Ticho was not so sure. When the children crowded onto the merry-go-round they looked at his broken, sprawling legs and did not want to ride him. They all said they wanted to ride a pretty horse that wasn't half smashed up. Ticho felt terribly humiliated, running around the circle without a rider. Only once in all that day and evening did he have a rider. That was when Mateo lifted a little girl onto his back because there was not another horse left for her. And she cried because she did not have a good horse to ride. She wanted to ride Mantequilla. No one seemed to notice anything wrong with Mantequilla at all.

The next day it was the same, and the day after that, and the day after that—all through the two weeks of the fair. Ticho grew very sad, and he did not feel like arguing with Mantequilla any more. After a day or two, Mantequilla stopped talking about Ticho's broken legs. Mantequilla did not talk any more about being at the head of the ring, either. And he began being very kind to Ticho.

"You know, Ticho," said Mantequilla, "you are just as beautiful as ever. That white paint looks all right on you, because you were spotted anyway. But it certainly looks awful on me, because butter-colored horses are not supposed to have white spots on them."

And somehow that made Ticho much sadder than if Mantequilla had kept on arguing about being more beautiful, and being at the head of the ring.

At last the fair in Mexico City ended. And Mateo and his father said they were going to take the merry-go-round and go to Guadalajara. All the little horses rather dreaded the trip, for they would have to travel shut up in big crates. So it was natural that none of them talked very much. But Ticho felt so sad and lonely now that he wished Mantequilla would start bragging again about being beautiful. But he didn't.

When Mateo and his father took Mantequilla off his little iron post, he just looked at Ticho and said: "Well, here we go again."

Then Mateo put him in the big crate, and came over to take Ticho off his post. But they did not put Ticho into the crate. They laid him down on the ground at one side, and went on and took Black Bolo off his post and put him into the crate.

Ticho's eyes grew wider and wider, and he breathed so hard that he got dust from the ground in his red, painted nostrils. For Mateo and his father were putting all the other little horses into the crates, and closing up the crates. And they had not put Ticho into any of them. He still lay on the ground among the confetti and the peanut shells and the bits of broken lumber.

"What shall we do with the broken one?" Mateo asked his father.

"Leave it there," said Mateo's father. "They will haul it away with the trash."

Ticho could not believe his ears. It could not be that they were going to leave him behind! But that is just what they were doing. They put the crates into the truck and drove away. And Ticho knew he would never see any of them again.

He would never again hear Mateo sing the songs that the calliope was playing. Never again would the children shout: "Oh, I want to ride the beautiful spotted pony!" Never again would he argue with Mantequilla.

Ticho shut his eyes and tried to imagine that he was running madly with the other little wooden horses. But all he could see behind his eyelids were the trucks driving away without him.

"I suppose Mantequilla *was* at the head of the ring," whispered Ticho. "After all, he was always just ahead of me. And he is beautiful. A butter-colored horse is much more unusual than a spotted horse. I have always known that. I have always known he is more beautiful than I am. But I wish I had told him so before he went away."

Just then some men came with a big flat truck and began gathering up all the scraps from where the fair had been. One of them picked Ticho up and tossed him against a pile of lumber, and began sweeping up the peanut shells and confetti.

Next a funny little truck drove up and a man got out. Then a nun with a kind face and black bonnet got out. Then they lifted out a little boy, who came walking toward Ticho. But Ticho had never before seen a little boy walk that way. He leaned on two crutches and his two thin little legs swung uselessly between them. He came straight to Ticho, and his face was bright and smiling.

"Hello, little horse," said the boy. "You look like a horse

from the merry-go-round. What are you doing here?"

"They left me behind," said Ticho. "My legs are broken and I am no good any more."

"Oh, dear me," said the little boy. He moved his crutches expertly and dropped down on the ground, and began examining Ticho's legs. "Yes, they are certainly broken," he said. "But that does not mean you are no good. I am a cripple, too, but there are lots of things I can do. I think Juan can fix your legs almost as good as new."

"But no one wants me now," said Ticho. "Children do not like to ride crippled horses."

"That is silly," said the boy. Then his eyes grew dreamy. "I'd love to have you. All the children at the orphanage would love you. And, after all, the merry-go-round people have thrown you away, so they don't want you any more."

Ticho was thinking what a nice boy this was, and wondering how he could be so happy when he was crippled.

"What is your name?" said the boy suddenly.

"Ticho."

"Well, look, Ticho. My name is Paco, and I live with the nuns at the orphanage. There are lots of children there, and we don't have much to play with. Would you like to come live with us? We'd be awfully good to you."

"I'd love that," said Ticho. And suddenly he felt happy again.

Paco looked around for the nun. She was pointing out bits of lumber that could be used at the orphanage; and the man who had come with them was putting them into the funny little truck.

"Sister Maria," called Paco, "will you ask them if we can have the little wooden horse?"

"Sure! Take him along!" said the men who were cleaning up the place where the fair had been. "Save us hauling him to the dump."

The nun walked over and smiled down at Paco, but she was talking to the men.

"Thank you," she said. "That is nice. The children will love him."

"Isn't he beautiful?" said Paco. "His name is Ticho."

"How do you know?" asked the nun.

"He told me," said Paco.

"Paco," said the nun, trying to be severe, "it is all right if you want to name him Ticho. But wooden horses cannot talk, so he could not possibly have told you that is his name. You must be careful about telling lies."

Paco blushed very red and looked at Ticho.

Ticho winked at him, and said, "Never mind. I know all about grown-ups."

So that is how it happened that Ticho went to live at the orphanage. All the children adored him at once. And none of them thought that Paco was lying when he said that Ticho talked to him, though a good many of them had never talked to wooden horses themselves.

Juan, the carpenter, fixed Ticho's legs with new nails, and put tape around them, and painted them dark red, the color of the rest of his legs. Ticho looked at them proudly and saw that they curved as beautifully as ever now, even if the scars did show.

They put him on a post in the shed in the garden, and all the children came every day to see him. Then one day Paco told him a great secret.

"Listen, Ticho," said Paco. "You liked running on the merry-go-round, didn't you?"

"Of course," said Ticho. "I love it here because everyone is so good to me, but I do miss the merry-go-round. There is not much point to your getting on my back if I am going to stand still. Even so, that is better than not having you get on my back at all."

"Well, here is a secret," said Paco. "Juan is going to build us a merry-go-round. His friend, the mechanic from the garage, is going to help him. They are trying now to get all the things they need to make a merry-go-round."

Ticho was so excited he could hardly stand it. Every night, as he dozed on his little post in the shed, he remembered the big merry-go-round and wished he could see Mantequilla again, and go racing round and round the circle with all the other little horses.

But now he was sure that this would be even better. For he loved Paco much more than he had loved Mateo. And there were all the other orphans, too—it would be much more fun to take them for rides, than to carry the children who had so many other things that the orphans did not have.

For months there was great excitement among the children at the orphanage. Juan and his friend, the mechanic, built the big round platform. They got a motor from a used-car dump, and they brought home several old automobile seats.

"You see, Ticho," Paco explained, "it would be nice to have all horses on the merry-go-round. But you are the only horse we have. Besides, some of the children are too crippled to sit on a horse, so the seats will be fine for them."

Then one day a marvelous thing happened. Juan came home with a wooden lion, just about Ticho's size. He was painted a lovely tawny color, and his face looked very fierce. His name was Leon (which is the Spanish word for "lion").

Leon told Ticho and Paco that once he and another lion had stood on the two sides of a big gate to guard it. But one day a truck crashed into the gate and knocked down the pedestals on which they stood, and smashed the other lion into bits. The foolish people thought Leon was no good without his mate, so they threw him away. And Juan had found him on the city dump. Leon was very grateful to Juan, and said he would be glad to act as a horse on the merry-go-round; although that was a poor fate for a fierce lion.

But pretty soon Leon, too, grew fond of the children. Paco put a fresh coat of paint on his face, and gave him a nice smile. And after that he was much happier.

It took a long time to make the merry-go-round. It could not be very grand, with just Ticho and Leon and a few car seats. But the children thought it was wonderful. At last the platform was ready, and the motor was working and could turn the platform in a circle. And now Juan began to make another wooden horse, so that Ticho would not be the only one.

By this time it was December, and Ticho knew the fair was there again, down by the Monument of the Revolution; and that Mateo and his father would be there, with the big fine merry-go-round, and all the wooden horses that were Ticho's friends. And Ticho thought about Mantequilla, too. He could almost hear the music of the calliope. There was nothing to make music with, on the little merry-go-round at the orphanage. But the children said that did not matter, for they would all sing and make their own music.

Juan kept putting off fastening Ticho and Leon to the posts he had fixed for them on the platform of the merry-go-round, because he wanted to finish the other little wooden horse.

Then one day Juan and Sister Maria and Paco drove off in the funny little truck. They were gone a long time. When they came back, Ticho was dozing on his post in the shed, and did not look up until he heard Juan drop something beside him.

"Hello, Ticho," said a voice beside him. "I see you are just as spotted as ever."

Ticho almost jumped off his post. He knew that voice! And, sure enough, there lay Mantequilla! And now Juan was coming into the shed with Black Bolo! Ticho could not believe his eyes!

"Mantequilla!" he cried. "What are you doing here? Surely that ragged tail was not enough to make them throw you away."

"I had another accident," Mantequilla explained. "A truck backed into our crate this morning and smashed Black Bolo and me. You should have seen us! They just threw us away, crate and all! Then your friends came and rescued us."

Ticho looked at him again, and saw that Mantequilla's beautiful arched neck was broken, and that Black Bolo's hind legs were crushed.

"You were right, Ticho," continued Mantequilla. "Remember when you told me I would not be much good without my head? That is what Mateo and his father thought."

"Never mind," said Ticho. "Juan can fix you both as good as new. Just look what he did for my legs. And they are making a merry-go-round for the orphan children, Mantequilla. We'll soon be running together again. And the children here —oh, you will love the children, Mantequilla!"

"Well," said Mantequilla, "I hope your friend Juan has some yellow paint. Even if he fixes my neck as well as he has your legs, it would still look funny with a ring of white paint around it."

"Juan will find yellow paint," Ticho told him. "He will make you as beautiful as ever." Then Ticho hesitated a moment, remembering this long year when he had missed Mantequilla so much. "Mantequilla, I think I ought to tell you—I always have thought a butter-colored horse is more beautiful than a spotted one."

"Well, bless my soul!" said Mantequilla.

Black Bolo began to laugh.

"The children here must be nice," said Black Bolo. "They have changed you so much, Ticho."

That was about the happiest Christmas the children at the orphanage had ever known. The merry-go-round was finished and set up in the garden, under a funny square tent that Juan and his friend, the mechanic, had made. The new little wooden horse that Juan had carved was rather funny looking, with his straight stubby legs and rope tail. But he was a jolly little horse with a comical face. His name was Juanito.

After dinner all the nuns came out into the garden to watch the children have their first ride on the new merry-go-round. Ticho and Mantequilla and Black Bolo and Juanito and Leon were all fixed on sturdy little posts. And the automobile seats were fastened at a comfortable angle. Then the children climbed on. Paco rode Ticho, for, after all, the merry-go-round was Paco's idea, and Ticho was the very first part of it.

Then Juan started the motor and the merry-go-round began to whirl. The little wooden horses and the lion and the automobile seats raced madly around the circle. And all the children laughed and sang at the tops of their voices. The nuns clapped their hands and laughed, too.

When the merry-go-round stopped, the children all climbed down and began changing seats for the next ride.

"Well," said Ticho, "it is fine to be racing again!"

"Yes," answered Mantequilla, "and you did very well

with your crippled legs. Of course, since I have four good legs it is only natural that I should stay at the head of the ring."

"The head of the ring?" shrieked Ticho. "How can you say you are at the head of the ring, when the red automobile seat is in front of you, and Juanito is in front of it, and Leon is in front of him, and—"

"Don't go over that again!" shouted Mantequilla. "You hate to admit I am at the head of the ring because you are envious of my beauty. Very few horses are the color of butter!"

"The color of butter, indeed!" said Ticho. "Of course, that color is all right, if one likes only one kind of paint. But very important horses should have more. It takes two kinds of paint to make a spotted horse!"

Then they both switched their silken tails and squeaked companionably on their little iron posts.

The Magic Baby Shoes

MANY years ago a little tree grew on the side of a mountain deep in the heart of Mexico. It was a sturdy little tree, and in the sunshine on the mountainside it grew and grew.

Down below, in the valley, lay a village. It was a gay little village with white adobe houses and gardens filled with bright flowers. The little tree loved to look down at the village in the green valley, and at the herds of white sheep and comical black and white goats that grazed on the green slopes.

He liked the small brown boys and girls who walked after the sheep and goats, and kept them from getting into the fields of corn and the vegetable gardens.

The little tree sometimes envied the fields and the sheep and the goats because they helped the people of the village so much. The little tree could do nothing but stand on the mountainside, with his roots deep in the soft earth.

He was very well acquainted with the people, for they often walked in the woods and he heard them talking. He heard more about them from the goats, for the sheep and goats often came into the woods and talked to the little tree. The sheep were rather stupid and had very little conversation, but the goats loved to gossip.

The little tree laughed the first time he saw the sheep running around with their wool clipped so short that they looked almost naked. Trees often laugh or cry, but most people think it is only the wind blowing through their leaves. Anyway, the little tree laughed.

He said: "What have you done with your lovely woolly coats that always looked so elegant?"

The sheep only shivered and looked foolish. Then the goats laughed, too. The Biggest Goat said: "Don't they look silly? And this happens to them every spring. The men of the village cut off their wool and make yarn of it. They weave the yarn into clothing and beautiful blankets. It takes them all year to make it all into blankets, and every market day they go down to the big town on the other side of the mountain, and sell the blankets. That is the only way they have to get money to buy the things they need in the town."

Then a small white goat with a peevish face spoke up. "And in the meantime," she said, "the sheep must run around naked all spring. It takes them a full year to grow a nice coat, and no sooner is it grown out than spring comes again, and again the people cut it all off."

"But they do cut it off in the spring," said the Biggest Goat, "when it is so warm they don't really need it."

"That makes no difference," answered the White Goat. "They look just as silly in the spring as they would at any other time."

But the little tree thought it was very kind of the people to take the wool only in the spring when it was warm, and never in winter when the cold winds crept over the mountains.

For many years the little tree stood on the mountainside. He learned to love the pleasant singing people of the village, and life seemed very quiet and uneventful. Then a tremendous thing happened to him.

One day a wood carver, who lived in the village, came into the woods. He had often been there before and the little tree knew him well. He was one of the few people who were able to talk to the animals and the trees, and he had spoken to the little tree many times, complimenting him on his growth. This day he came and sat down beside the little tree and looked at him a long time. The little tree rustled in a friendly manner, and asked the wood carver what he was thinking about.

The wood carver said, "Little Tree, I have news for you. I hope you will not mind too much, but I am going to cut you down."

The little tree was brave and tried not to look startled. But he shivered so that his teeth chattered—that is, his leaves rattled.

"You see," the wood carver went on, "some trees can stand on the mountainside all their lives. But you are such a fine tree that you must do your share of work in the world."

The little tree asked in a small voice: "Are you going to cut me up for wood to make a fire, as other men have done to some of my brothers?"

"No," said the wood carver. "That isn't a bad fate, but yours is much better. The trees that are burned don't die. They live on in the warmth they make. And when that is gone, they live on in a wisp of smoke and an added fragrance on the air that goes on forever. But you will live on in a new shape. I am going to take the wood that is your heart and make it into an image of the Christ Child, to put in the niche in our church. So you see, you will live forever in the very image of the Christ Child."

The little tree sighed. "That is very nice. Only I wish I could be a big saint, so I could do something to help the people of the village. A baby is such a helpless thing. I know. I've seen them carried on their mothers' backs through the woods."

"But the Christ Child was the greatest saint of all," the wood carver told him, "for He was holy even when He was a

baby. You will see. You will like being an image of the Christ
Child."

Then the wood carver picked up his axe and began to chop
the little tree down. It did not hurt as much as the tree had
expected, for he was busy wondering how it would feel to be
an image in the church, instead of a tree on the mountainside.

It was quite a while before he was actually changed. The
wood carver took a long time to make the image. It was not a
very large image—not quite so large as a real baby. But the
carver took great pains with his work, and the image was
very beautiful. Now, some wood carvers are careless with
the bodies of their images, but this one wasn't. The lovely pale
wood was cut to the exact shape of a baby's body. The little
arms curved just so, and each little hand had five tiny fingers.
But when he came to make the feet the wood carver had some
difficulty. The legs were fine, but he did not know how to
carve beautiful toes, and he did not want to make ugly ones.
So, in the end, he made the feet just solid, with no toes at all.

When the image was finished the women of the village
made a fine baby dress for him. They sewed lace on it, and
around the hem they embroidered, in bright colors, a row
of tiny sheep and goats and birds. This pleased the little
image, for it reminded him of his old friends on the mountainside.

Then the children of the village gathered around to look
at the image. He loved the children and felt very much at
home with them as they admired him.

They said, "He is so beautiful. His face looks ready to

smile, and his hands are as pretty as baby Pedro's. But his feet—look at them! How sad! His feet are not beautiful at all —because the wood carver doesn't know how to carve toes!"

And another said: "Couldn't the shoemaker make him some sandals to cover his feet?"

Then everyone looked at his own feet. Their sandals were only heavy soles, with strips of leather across the top, and did not cover their toes at all. So again they all said: "How sad!"

"I can make him some sandals, with the tops all leather," the shoemaker told them, "so they will cover his toes—or rather cover the place where he has no toes. They will be special sandals. But after all, we should make special shoes for El Niño Santo."

(You see, these people were Mexicans so they spoke Spanish, and *El Niño Santo* is Spanish for "The Holy Child.") When the new little image heard them call him El Niño Santo, he suddenly realized that now he was neither a tree on the mountainside, nor a block of wood in the wood carver's house. He was an image of the Holy Child! And his home now was in the very heart of the village.

By the time he got through thinking about how wonderful this was, the shoemaker had finished his shoes. They were lovely shoes of very soft white leather, and the women tied them on his little wooden feet with blue ribbon.

Then the people carried him to the church and laid him in the special niche for which he had been made. But the wood carver had been so interested in making the little image beautiful that he had forgotten to be careful about his size. And now they found the niche was a little small for him, and his feet stuck over the edge just a tiny bit. But nobody minded, for now his feet, in their little white baby shoes with the gay blue ribbons, were quite as beautiful as the rest of him. When they held baby Pedro up to look at him in the niche, Pedro leaned over and kissed the little white feet.

Everybody smiled and said: "How nice that the niche is a little small for him. He is closer to us this way."

Now the little image was not put in the most important place. He had a little niche along the side of the nave, where the people passed by him and paused to speak to him on their way to the altar. Behind the altar, in the most important place in the church, was a huge image of Jesus on the Cross. There the people knelt and prayed. But when they walked by the little image of the Baby they smiled and kissed his feet. That is the way it should be. It was only after Jesus was on the Cross that people knew He was God. When He was a baby He was just Mary's little baby—one of the people. This was much cozier.

The little Niño Santo was very happy in the church. The people were happy, too. And it seemed that life might go on this way until the end of time. But the very next year things changed. Before the winter was well over the weather turned very hot, and the Niño Santo, looking out through the open door of the church, could see great clouds of dust blowing through the streets. And now the people came more often to the church to pray, and their faces looked worried and sad.

The spring passed, and it was time for the rains of summer. But no rain came. The Niño Santo could see the sheep and goats wandering through the streets, because there was no grass on the hillsides for them to eat. They looked thin and sad. And the people looked more and more worried.

Then one day the wood carver came into the church to pray. When he had prayed before the big image of Jesus on the Cross, he stopped in front of the niche of the Niño Santo.

"Well, little Niño Santo," said the wood carver, "you should be glad that I cut down the little tree and made you from the wood that was its heart. For if you were a tree on the mountainside now, you would probably die. The rains have not come, and the corn cannot grow, and there is no grass for the goats and sheep to eat. If the rain does not come in a few days there will be nothing for any of us to eat this winter. And if the rain never comes again the trees on the mountainside will die, too."

"This is terrible!" said the Niño Santo. "Can't you work in the fields and make the corn grow? Can't you feed the sheep and goats something else if there is no grass?"

"There is nothing else to feed them," answered the wood carver. "And no amount of work will make the corn grow if there is no rain."

"Let me think about this," said the Niño Santo. "I can remember when I was a tree, and now I am an image of the Christ Child. Surely, with all that, I should be able to think of something."

The wood carver kissed the Niño Santo's feet in their little white shoes with the gay blue ribbons, and went away. The Niño Santo looked at his little white shoes, and then suddenly he had an idea.

"Why, these are special shoes," he thought. "I am not only an image of the Christ Child, but I have special shoes. No other image in the world has shoes like mine. I do believe I can walk in them. If I can just get out of my niche and take a walk I think I can do something about this matter of the rain."

That night, when everyone in the village was in bed and sound asleep, the little Niño Santo got out of his niche. And, sure enough, he could walk in the little white shoes with their gay blue ribbons. He ran out into the fields where nothing was growing, and his feet sank deep into the dust that should have been soft moist earth. He called down to the grains of corn planted deep in the dusty earth.

"Grains of corn," he said, "why do you not put up your sprouts and grow, so the people and the goats and the sheep will have food to eat?"

The corn answered faintly: "We cannot grow without the rain. Send us rain and we will make the biggest crop of corn the village has ever had."

Then the Niño Santo said to the sheep, "Look at your coats! You have done nothing about growing more wool since you were clipped in the spring. Why don't you get busy and grow some wool, so the people of the village will have yarn to make their blankets to sell in the market town?"

The Oldest Sheep answered: "I don't know. The wool just doesn't seem to grow. This has never happened to us before."

But the wise Big Black Goat said, "They cannot grow wool because they are hungry. A sheep must be well fed if he is to grow wool. Make the grass and the corn grow, and they will raise the finest crop of wool the village has ever had."

"And you," said the Niño Santo to the goat, "you goats aren't doing your share either. What about the milk you are supposed to give the people? All the children look starved because there isn't enough milk."

"It takes green grass and a bit of corn to make milk," said the Big Black Goat. "Give us food and we will make plenty of milk for the whole village."

The little Niño Santo thought about all these answers for a bit, and then he said: "Well, it all seems to be a matter of rain. If the rains would come everything would be all right."

He looked up at the sky, and there were millions of stars and the big yellow moon, but no clouds. And the stars cannot send rain. It takes clouds to make rain. He looked at the sky very carefully, and just over the top of the mountain he saw one lazy little white cloud, lying asleep.

"You, up there in the sky!" shouted the Niño Santo. "You lazy little cloud, what do you mean by sleeping all these weeks when you should be bringing rain so the corn and grass can grow, and the goats can make milk, and the sheep can make wool, and the people of the village can go on living!"

The lazy white cloud yawned and did not want to answer.

But because the Niño Santo was the image of the Christ Child he had to pay attention to him.

"Well," said the lazy little cloud—and anyone would know he was just making excuses—"we clouds thought we should have a vacation. We don't want to work."

"But everyone must work," said the Niño Santo. "If you don't send rain to keep the earth moist and fruitful, there will be no morning dew for you to draw up to make new clouds. And then you clouds yourselves will die. Now run along and call your family, and bring the rain at once."

So the lazy little cloud shook himself and slipped back over the mountain. And pretty soon there he came again with all his family following him. The father and mother clouds were huge and black and filled with rain. The big brothers and sisters had brought their lightning with them. And they began to have a fine time throwing their lightning at the mountain tops, while the thunder shrieked with laughter. Then a few drops of rain fell, and the goats and sheep kicked up their heels and ran wildly around the fields, hunting for the first blade of grass that might put its head through the earth. And the grains of corn, planted deep in the fields, sighed with contentment and began waking up their little sprouts and getting them ready to grow.

The Niño Santo was quite pleased to see how well everyone was obeying him. His night's work was done now, so he hurried back to the church. The first drops of rain had wet the dust and some of it stuck to his little white shoes with the gay blue ribbons. But he did not notice that. He went back and climbed into his niche and fell fast asleep.

The next morning the people were very happy because it was raining and already the dry earth was coming to life. Everything was going to be all right now. That day the wood carver came again to the church and stopped in front of the Niño Santo, and looked at his little white shoes in wonder.

"That's very strange," said the wood carver. "Look at his shoes. They are quite dirty. The children must have been kissing his feet when their faces were dirty. But no, that is mud, and no child would have mud on his face. It is very strange!"

The wood carver shook his head and walked away, and the Niño Santo smiled to himself because of his secret. Only he knew why his shoes were dirty.

Every day the cloud family brought the rain, and the corn grew tall, and the grass was thick and green, and the sheep and the goats were getting fat again. But, after a few months, the Niño Santo noticed that again the people were looking worried, and that the sheep and goats were spending as much time standing in the shelter of the houses in the village as they spent out on the mountainside eating grass.

So when the wood carver came again and stopped to smile at him, the Niño Santo said: "Tell me, wood carver, why are the people looking so worried again? Aren't those clouds bringing you enough rain?"

"That is just the trouble," answered the wood carver.

"They are bringing too much rain. The crops are ready to harvest, and the men cannot go into the fields because there is so much rain and mud."

"Dear me," said the Niño Santo, "I hadn't thought of that. But do not worry, I shall do something about it."

"What can you do?" said the wood carver. "You are only a little wooden image."

"You forget," answered the Niño Santo with great dignity, "that I am made from the heart of a living tree, and am an image of the Christ Child. Since you made me, you should be the last person in the world to forget that. Also, I have special shoes."

But the wood carver only shook his head and went away, still looking worried.

That night the Niño Santo again climbed down from his niche and went out to the fields.

"You, Clouds," said the Niño Santo, "you are working too hard. You must go away and let the sun shine for a bit. You really must learn to use better judgment about your work. It is necessary for everyone to do his share of work in this world. But you must rest sometimes and give other people a chance. Go away now and wait until we need rain again."

So the clouds scurried as fast as they could across the sky and the stars came out and shone happily, cleaning up the sky for the sun to come in the morning.

Then the sheep and the goats came romping into the fields of grass. They laughed and shouted to their friend, the Niño Santo.

"Thank you," they said. "It was fun to play in the rain when it first came. But we have grown tired of it now, and are happy to have the starlight, and to know that tomorrow the sun will shine."

"Well, someone has to look after the village," said the Niño Santo. "It seems that it takes so many things to make the world go smoothly. From now on I shall visit the fields regularly, and see that there is exactly the right amount of rain and the right amount of sunshine. By the way, Sheep, I see that you have done very well in your wool growing. You all have fine coats now, and should give the people a great deal of wool next spring."

"Yes," said the Big Black Goat. "It will be the biggest cutting of wool in years. And that reminds me of something else. All the looms in the town are getting lazy. I have heard the people talking about it. It seems that they work so slowly that it is hard to get all the wool woven into blankets in time for the market days."

So the Niño Santo went to see the looms. He went first to the biggest house where there were three looms.

"What is the matter with you?" said the Niño Santo. "The goats tell me that you are very slow and do not make the weaving even, so the blankets are not so beautiful as they should be."

"How can we help it?" said the biggest loom. "We are only pieces of wood and we are old and tired."

"Just pieces of wood?" said the Niño Santo. "That is a stupid thing to say. Don't you remember that you were once living trees? It is simply that your job now is being a loom, just as my job is being an image of the Christ Child. Remember when you were a tree, and weave the blankets as carefully as you used to weave patterns of sunshine and shade on the floor of the forest."

"That's right," said the old loom. "I had almost forgotten. It is really more fun to weave blankets because they last for many years, and the patterns of shadow and sunshine last only a few hours. We will be more careful in the future."

By the time the Niño Santo had called on all the looms in the town it was almost morning, and he had to hurry to get back to his niche in the church. That day the wood carver again came to the church, and again he stopped in front of the niche of the Niño Santo.

"The sun is shining today," he said happily, "and we can harvest the corn." Then he looked at the Niño Santo's feet. "Look at your shoes!" cried the wood carver. "How on earth do they get so muddy when you lie all the time in your niche?"

Just then a ray of sunshine slipped through the window of the church and fell across the niche, and the Niño Santo smiled. The wood carver saw the smile, and suddenly he knew exactly how the Niño Santo got his shoes so dirty. He ran out into the village and told all the people that it was the Niño Santo who had brought the rains and then sent them away, and had made the corn grow tall. And the people came to thank him, and to kiss his feet in their little white shoes with the gay blue ribbons. And everyone was very happy.

All this happened a hundred years ago. But the Niño Santo still looks after the fields, and blesses the looms, and encourages the sheep to grow wool. And now the village is known far and wide as the town where the corn is tallest, where the goats give most milk, where the sheep grow the best wool, and where the most beautiful blankets in the whole country are made.

The people of the town know very well whom to thank for all this. The little Niño Santo is everyone's friend. And every year on his birthday—that is Christmas Day, you know—they give him a new white dress with lace sewed on it, and around the bottom is embroidered, in bright colors, a row of tiny sheep and goats and birds. But the best present that he gets on every birthday, is a new pair of white leather shoes, tied on his little wooden feet with new blue ribbons.

Not very long ago, some people came from the market town to visit the village and buy some of the famous blankets made there. And they went to visit the church and stood in front of the Niño Santo.

"That is a very beautiful Christ Child," said the lady. "But look at his shoes! How dirty they are!"

"Yes," said the man disapprovingly, "it is because the people here kiss his feet every day and get his white shoes dirty. They should put up a sign that no one may kiss his feet without the consent of the priest."

The Niño Santo smiled, and the lady saw the smile.

"Look," said the lady, "the way the sunshine falls across

his face it looks as though he were smiling!"

Then the people of the village laughed. These visitors could not understand, but they who lived in the village knew the secret of their rich fields and their fine weaving. They knew about the smile of the Niño Santo, and about his dirty little white shoes, tied with gay blue ribbon.

Tlacuache the Saint

ONCE upon a time in the Valley of Mexico, there was a great drought.

Of course, no one expected the rains to fall during the long months of the dry season. In this season only the flowers that can draw their moisture from deep in the ground continue to bloom. And there are many such flowers. But even in those dry months sometimes there is just a little rain. Then in June the heavy rains come, and the whole earth bursts into bloom, and all the animal people are very happy.

But one year, all through the long dry season there was not a drop of rain. The animal people in the woods were not worried, though, for they said that soon it would be June and then the water would come, and the world would be green and beautiful again. But June came and there was no rain. After a while everyone began to worry about it. But worry never helps a bad situation, and there was still no rain. Then the animal people were not only worried, but they were hungry.

For of course you understand that the animal people who live in the woods cannot live unless the rains come, and the fruits and nuts and grasses grow. The squirrels had eaten all their old nuts, and there were no new ones on the trees. The rabbits could scarcely find enough roots and green leaves to keep them from starving. And even the tigers and the coyotes were hungry, for all the little animals they liked to eat were so thin and starved that there was no use in eating them.

The whole summer passed, and the dry winter months came again, and still there was no rain. The earth got drier and drier, and browner and browner. And the animal people got hungrier and hungrier, and more and more worried. The rabbits went down to the fields and gardens of the human people in the town, to see if they could find some lettuce or carrots. But the gardens and fields were dry, too, and there was nothing there to eat. The foxes and the coyotes went down to the town to try to steal chickens from the pens of the human people. But the chickens were so thin and hungry that they were not worth eating. And the dogs of the town were so thin and hungry that they did not even bother to chase the coyotes and foxes. There was nothing left for the dogs to protect, so it was not worth the effort to bark.

One day the coyote, who is the wisest of all the animal people, called a meeting of everyone who lived in the woods, so that they could decide what to do. Some of the birds and small animals were a little worried about that convention. They were not quite sure they would be safe sitting in conference with tigers and coyotes and foxes.

The widow rabbit, Concha Conejo (you understand that *conejo* is the Spanish word for "rabbit") mentioned her fears to the tlacuache.

I cannot tell you what tlacuache means in English, as there is no English word for it. But the tlacuache is a little gray and white animal who looks quite a lot like a raccoon. He has rather a pretty face and his coarse hair is long and thick. But his long tail is very ugly, for it hasn't a single hair and always looks dirty. The tlacuache never looks at his own tail, because he is ashamed of it. When he drinks from a stream he sees only his pretty face, and he pretends that is all anyone can see.

Anyway, when Concha Conejo told Tlacuache that she was worried about the convention, he sat down and scratched his stomach and thought about it.

"I don't know," said Tlacuache, "I am not much afraid

of the fox, for I am almost as big as he is—if you don't count his long legs. But I must say I should not like to sit next to the coyote nor the tiger."

Just then Sancho Zorro the Fox came along. (You must know that *zorro* is the Spanish word for "fox.") He had such sharp ears that he had heard Concha and Tlacuache talking. And he thought what they said was very funny, for Sancho has the greatest sense of humor of all the animal people.

"Hello, friends," said Sancho. "Are you coming to the animal convention in the heart of the woods tonight?"

"Oh, yes! yes!" said Tlacuache importantly.

"Well, I don't know," said Concha. "I'm thinking about it."

"Ah, yes," said Sancho, "I heard you thinking." Then he threw back his head and laughed. "Don't worry, Concha. I want you to fatten on good green leaves before I eat you. And as for you, Tlacuache, I doubt if even the tiger would bother with all that hair of yours for the sake of the mouthful of bones he'd find under it. Better come to the meeting and see what we can do about the rain."

"Of course we're coming," said Tlacuache crossly. "Is it so funny that people discuss important matters?"

So that night all the animal people met in the heart of the Great Woods and talked about the drought. The badger suggested that they might dig a ditch from the river to the woods, so that the water from the river might come to make the woods green again.

"But that will not work," said Raul the Coyote, "for I have

observed that water never runs up the side of a mountain, but always down."

"Besides," said the beaver, "there is scarcely enough water left in the river to make the reeds grow. The river would not give its water to the woods, even if the mountain were down hill."

"No," said the tiger, "there is nothing for us to do, but to persuade the clouds to send us the rain."

"But how can we persuade the clouds," said Valentin Venado the Deer, "since we never see a cloud these days, except when one floats up from the gulf to laugh at us?"

Just then the crow arrived. He was very late and he arrived quite out of breath. He perched on the lowest limb of a tree and gave a loud caw to attract the attention of the animals.

"Caw! Caw! Hear ye! Hear ye!" said the crow. "I have just come from a visit to all the villages of the human people in the valley. I have been observing what the human people are doing about the lack of rain. I thought it might give us an idea."

Everybody began talking at once.

"Tell us! What are they doing?"

"The human people are wise. What are they doing about the drought?"

"Do the human people know where to find the clouds?"

"If you will keep still I will tell you," said the crow impatiently. "I saw that in all the villages the people are making processions. In each town all the people go to the church. They take one of their saints and put him on a litter and carry him through the town, singing praises to him, and begging him to bring the clouds and the rain."

Everybody began talking at once.

"A good idea. The human people are wise."

"Why didn't we think of that?"

"We will make a procession, too."

"Just a minute," said the gray squirrel. "What saint is it they carry? What saint can make the rains come?"

"It doesn't seem to make any difference," said the crow. "In some towns it was one saint, in other towns another. Every town seems to have its own saint."

"That's just it," said Raul the Coyote. "Every town has its own saint. But we have no saint. How can we make a procession without a saint?"

Everybody was silent at once.

Some of them were wondering why they did not have a saint of their own, and others were wondering what they could do about the rain without a saint. The tiger walked up and down and lashed his tail about. The coyote sat still and twitched his ears. And the deer went and rubbed his antlers against a tree, because he thought that would help him to think better.

Then suddenly Tlacuache sat up and thumped his tail on the ground.

"I know!" said Tlacuache. "It's very easy. Why don't we get a saint of our own and make a procession?"

Everybody began talking at once.

"Of course, why didn't we think of that before?"

"But where will we find a saint?"

"What does a saint look like?"

"The saints of the human people," said the crow, "are made of wood, and they are made to look like people."

"Then our saint," said Raul the Coyote, "should be an animal. But none of us can make an animal saint out of wood."

"Except the woodpecker," said the deer. "He might do it if we gave him time enough."

"We should all starve to death," said Sancho Zorro the Fox, "if we wait for the woodpecker to make a saint with his beak."

"Well, I should think," said Tlacuache, "that a live saint would do better than a wooden saint. Couldn't we find a live animal saint?"

"Silly," said the crow, "there aren't any live saints."

"Let's have an election," said Sancho Zorro with a grin. "We'll elect a saint from among ourselves. We are all so good I am sure any one of us would make a fine saint."

Sancho meant that for a joke, but all the animal people thought it a wonderful idea. And they all began talking at once about whom they should choose to be the saint. Some of the timid animals suggested the tiger, because he was the fiercest animal in the woods and they thought it would please him. But Concha Conejo said that, personally, she did not think they should have a saint of whom anyone was afraid.

"Why not elect Tlacuache?" said Raul the Coyote. "It was

his idea in the first place. And certainly no one is afraid of Tlacuache."

"Also," said Valentin Venado the Deer, "he is small and it would be much easier to carry him on a litter than to carry the tiger."

So they elected Tlacuache to be the saint. And everyone except Sancho Zorro the Fox went to work at once to make a litter to carry him in the procession. Sancho sat down beside a tree and laughed. And of course, Tlacuache did not help make the litter because he was the saint. He sat on the other side of the tree, and washed his face and hands and practiced looking saintly.

At last the litter was made, and they chose Valentin Venado the Deer, and his wife, Vera Venada, to carry it, because they were taller than the other animals, and very graceful. The litter was laid across their backs and they practiced walking slowly side by side for a bit. Then the animal people lifted Tlacuache to the litter, and they all set out walking in a procession through the woods and high up the mountainside.

As they walked they did not forget to sing praises to the new saint. They lifted up their voices in a great animal chant as they marched, and each tried to think of a nicer thing than the others to say to their saint.

"Beautiful Saint Tlacuache!"

"Good Saint Tlacuache, with the lovely pointed nose!"

"Kind Saint Tlacuache, with four velvet paws!"

"Great Saint Tlacuache, with fur like a gray forest!"

Tlacuache sat on the litter and listened to them. And his heart swelled with pride. He had always known he had rather a pretty face, but he had no idea before that he was so marvelous. He sat up straighter on the litter and lifted his face proudly.

"Beautiful Saint Tlacuache, bring us the rain!" chanted the animals.

Up on the top of the mountain a little white cloud was fast asleep, but all the noise in the woods woke him up. He drifted higher in the sky to see what was going on. When he saw the animals marching in procession and the proud little tlacuache sitting on the litter, he began to laugh. He laughed so hard that he puffed up into quite a big cloud. And his cloud brothers, down over the gulf, heard him laughing and came rolling up over the mountains to see what it was all about. So that after a while the sky was filled with all sizes of clouds, watching the animals make a procession for Saint Tlacuache.

"Good Saint Tlacuache, with lovely round black eyes!"

"Pretty Saint Tlacuache, with teeth like stars!"

But instead of thinking about how he was going to bring the rain to the people who were worshipping him, Tlacuache began to think more and more about how beautiful he was. By that time he was sure he really was a saint. But instead of begging the clouds to bring rain, he listened for new words telling how good and beautiful he was. He looked around to see who was singing the loudest. He saw Concha Conejo hopping along breathlessly beside the litter, but saying nothing.

"Concha Conejo!" said Tlacuache sternly. "Why aren't you singing? Can't you think of anything good to say about me?"

"Oh, yes, indeed, Tlacuache—I mean Saint Tlacuache," said Concha. "Beautiful Saint Tlacuache, with the pretty pointed ears."

Up in the sky a big black cloud rolled over his neighbors to get a better look.

"Look at Tlacuache!" laughed the big black cloud. "He thinks he really is a saint. I wonder what it is the animals want so much that they are going to all this trouble? Whatever it is, their new saint isn't trying to get it for them."

That was the truth. Tlacuache had forgotten completely why he had been made a saint, because he was so interested in hearing himself praised. Everyone seemed to be singing praises and looking very solemn, except Sancho Zorro who had run on ahead and was sitting beside the path laughing as the procession approached. Tlacuache sat very straight and stared at Sancho as they passed him.

"What is the matter, Sancho Zorro?" said Tlacuache sternly. "Are you so stupid you can think of nothing to say about your saint?"

"Ah, no," Sancho Zorro leaped to his feet and made a deep bow and put on a very solemn look. "Hail, Saint Tlacuache, with the dirty hairless tail!" chanted Sancho.

Tlacuache tried not to look round at his tail, but he did and was very angry. He whirled around on the litter and screamed at Sancho.

"What's that? What did you say to me?"

"I said, 'Hail, Saint Tlacuache, with the dirty hairless tail!'" said Sancho.

Then Tlacuache was very angry. The idea of talking that way to a saint! No one should mention the hairless tail of a saint! Tlacuache began to jump up and down on the litter, and he shook it so hard that Valentin and Vera, the two deer, dropped it. And Tlacuache fell in a heap between them. Then he got to his feet and thumped the ground angrily with his tail.

"You should be ashamed," he said, "to say such things to a saint! Just for that, I will not ride on the litter any more!"

All the other animal people began to beg Tlacuache to get back on the litter and try to bring them the rain. Tlacuache remembered then why he had been made a saint, but he was so angry he did not care whether it rained or not.

"You must say you are sorry, Sancho!" screamed Tlacu-- ache. "If you want to talk about my tail you may say it is long and strong and beautiful. But you must not call it a dirty hairless tail!"

"Hail, Saint Tlacuache," said Sancho, making a more solemn face than ever, "Hail, Saint Tlacuache with the long strong tail that has much dirt but no hair! There, is that better, Tlacuache?"

Then Tlacuache was so angry he could do nothing but jump up and down and thump his tail on the ground.

Up in the sky the clouds began to laugh. They laughed so hard that the big black clouds spilled some of the rain they were carrying, and the great drops fell down to the forest. The animal people felt the drops of rain, and they looked up and saw the sky filled with clouds.

"Look! Look!" they all cried at once. "Look at the clouds! The rains are coming!"

They forgot all about Tlacuache and his anger. They stopped trying to persuade him to get back on the litter. Instead, they were all watching the clouds and begging them to send more rain. A cool little wind rippled through the forest and ran up toward the top of the mountain.

"Come on now, Clouds," said the wind. "You have had a long vacation. It is time you gave them the water now."

So all the big clouds in the sky opened and sent the rain pouring into the forest, washing the trees and soaking the dry earth. Then every one of the animals—the tiger, the coyote, the deer, the crow—every single animal thought each of his own special part of the forest, and they all wanted to go home. They rushed away in all directions, lifting their heads to the rain.

Tlacuache sat beside a tree, watching the leaves dance in the downpour of rain, and suddenly he felt very sad.

"If only I had stayed on the litter and asked for the rain," he said, "instead of bothering with Sancho Zorro, I would have had the credit for bringing the rain. Then I might have been a saint all my life." He sighed and became angry again. "It is all the fault of Sancho Zorro the Fox, for talking about my hairless tail!"

"Oh, no, Tlacuache," said a little voice beside him.

He looked around and there sat Concha Rabbit under a bush.

"No, Tlacuache," said Concha. "It was your own fault, for being so vain. You let a little praise go to your head."

And Concha, too, hopped away into the forest. Tlacuache sat still beside the tree for a little while. Then he began to think about the roots and berries that would grow now that the rains had come.

"Oh, well," he said, "that litter was uncomfortable anyway. I'd much rather walk on my own four velvet paws."

Popo and the Coyote

OF ALL the dogs who lived on the big hacienda in Mexico, old Popo was the oldest. He had lived so long that his grandson, Brujo, was an old dog, and Brujo's granddaughter Mali was now the best dog on the hacienda. With the help of Brujo and two other young dogs, Mali now did most of the work of guarding the sheep and the goats and the turkeys.

Old Popo still had his special place in the shed where he

slept at night, and every evening the human people of the hacienda gave him a big bowl of food. But Popo did not like his food much these days. When he was a young dog, and worked at looking after the sheep and turkeys and guarding the hacienda, he was fed great pieces of raw meat and huge juicy bones to tear with his strong teeth. Now his food was a bowl of gruel with a little ground meat mixed in it.

"Poor old Popo," said Carmela, the cook, when she brought him his supper. "Poor old Popo. He has no teeth now, but here is nice soft food for him."

Popo knew they meant to be kind but it made him very unhappy, for he felt that he was no longer important to the human people of the hacienda. Mali was the important dog now, and they had all forgotten the days when Popo was the leader and the one they could always depend on.

One day Popo was taking a walk across the fields, and when he got tired he lay down to rest beside a big maguey plant. The ground was soft and fresh, and he liked the earth smell and the feel of the hot sun as it shone on him and warmed his bones. It was very pleasant. Lying there in the sun Popo felt as young and strong as he had ever been. He wondered why he had got into the habit of staying at home instead of following Guillermo, the boy who watched the sheep, and why he did not howl for a bone when it was feeding time in the evening. The way he felt now, lying there in the sun, he was quite sure he could do all the things he had done when he was a young dog.

"Why, it is probably all my own fault," thought Popo.

"It is just that I have grown lazy, and the human family believes that I am too old to work. Tomorrow I shall begin doing my own work again."

The next morning Popo got up very early and went down across the little meadow to the sheds where the sheep stayed at night. Mali and Oro, the beautiful young collie, were urging the sheep through the gate and starting them out across the meadow toward the grazing land on the lower hills. Popo ran after some of the stragglers and turned them back toward the flock. It was good to be working again.

Mali saw him, and as soon as she could she came to him. She was so busy that she could stop only a moment, but she looked annoyed with him.

"Go home, Popo," said Mali, "you are too old for this work. We are taking the sheep all the way to the river these days, and it is a long hard journey. Go home and rest."

"I did this work long before you were born," said Popo peevishly. "I know perfectly well how far it is to the meadows by the river."

Then Guillermo saw Popo. He laughed, and called him and petted him a little.

"Good old Popo," said Guillermo, "you have been a good dog to help get the sheep started. Now go on home."

But Popo did not go home. He circled out far to the side of the flock and kept out of Guillermo's sight until the sheep were out in the hills eating the green grass, all the time moving on toward the meadows down by the river. By the time Guillermo saw Popo again they were so far from the hacienda that Guillermo let him stay.

But Mali was right. The river meadows were a long way from the house, and the day was very hot. It had been a long time since Popo had run after the sheep, and before the morning was half over he was so tired that he felt quite dizzy. He knew he was a help to Mali and Oro because at least he could watch one side of the flock, but he could not run very fast any more. And Mali was cross with him.

"I know this was your job once, Popo," said Mali, "but now I am responsible for the sheep, and although you are a little help, it is not enough to make up for my worrying about you. Today I must not only watch the sheep, but I must worry about you."

"You have less to think about than usual," snapped Popo, "for I am here to help with the sheep. I do not deny that you are the head dog now, but at least I can help. And you need not worry about me. I looked after the sheep for many years, and no one has ever had to worry about me."

But at eleven o'clock when they at last reached the big meadows by the river, Popo was not only hot and thirsty as he had expected to be, but he was so tired his legs felt shaky. Mali and Oro ran down to the river to drink, and Popo ran with them. Or rather, he ran after them, for he could not run fast enough to catch up. When he reached the river Mali and Oro were already turning back toward the flock of sheep grazing on the rolling meadow.

Popo went to the edge of the water. It smelled cool and fresh, but it rushed past him so fast that it made him dizzy.

So he sat down for a moment to let his head clear. He was afraid if he tried to drink when he was so dizzy he might fall into the river. As he sat thinking about this, he remembered how he used to plunge into the river and swim when they came with the sheep to the lower meadow. He looked at the rushing river, and knew that he could not swim in it. He could only swim in the brook that ran through the home meadow now.

But after a while he felt better, and he stepped carefully to the edge of the water and drank. Just then he heard Mali calling him. But he did not bother to answer her because he was drinking. Then Mali came dashing back to the river.

"Popo!" cried Mali. "Why didn't you answer me? I was worried. I thought maybe you had fallen into the river."

"And what if I should fall into the river?" growled Popo. "I can swim, can't I? I used to swim this river before you were born—before your grandfather was born!"

Mali laughed. "Of course you did," she said, "but that is not to say you can swim it now."

"Go mind the sheep," said Popo gruffly, "or you will soon have the job of pulling the lambs out of the river." And he walked stiffly up the bank on his shaking legs.

He climbed to a knoll and lay down in the shade of a maguey and looked out over the countryside. Down below he could see the long sunny road that led from the hacienda to town. Then Popo began to dream, although he was completely awake. He remembered how he used to watch the sheep on these hills long ago when he was young and strong, and how, in the evening he would watch for the burros to come home from town along the long sunny road.

Popo had always been very friendly with the burros, and he had one special friend among them. Her name was Chucha. That is the name that Celestino called her, and all the other burros and animal people of the hacienda used to call her Chucha, too. She was still one of the best burros on the hacienda, but everyone had forgotten her name—everyone but Popo. Celestino had gone away and now Miguel took care of the burros, and he called her Abuela (which is Spanish for "grandmother"). All the other burros referred to her simply as The Oldest Burro, and they, too, called her Abuela. Only Popo remembered that her name had once been Chucha.

Just then there was a commotion among the sheep, and Popo heard Guillermo shouting. He jumped up and ran toward them, and saw that some of the sheep were going as fast as they could run, down the gully to the south. The sheep were never allowed there, for the gully was full of swamps where they might get lost. Popo saw Mali and Oro going after them and he ran, too, to help them. He ran as fast as he could, but he did not catch up with the leaders until they were almost to the swamp. And by that time Mali and Oro were there and turning them back.

Popo stopped because he realized that his heart was beating so fast he could hardly breathe, and his legs were shaking so hard that he knew he could not possibly help chase the sheep back to the high ground of the meadow. He limped painfully to the shadow of a small tree, and there he fell down and lay gasping. He could hear the voices of the other dogs, but they sounded very far away. Then Mali came to him. He could not see her because he could not open his eyes. Her voice sounded far away, but he could feel that she was quite near.

"Popo," said Mali. "What is the matter, Popo?"

He tried to answer because he did not want Mali to think he was so tired. But he had no voice, and he just lay still. Mali said nothing more, and Popo did not hear her go away. In fact he did not hear anything for a long time, for he went to sleep. So he did not know that Mali hurried the sheep back to the meadow as fast as they could go, and then went and told Guillermo about Popo.

It is very difficult for dogs to tell such things to human people, for although the dogs learn many words of our language, there are very few people who can understand the language of the dogs. But Mali and Guillermo understood each other. So when Mali came to him and whined and looked toward the swamp, Guillermo knew something was wrong. He thought maybe one of the sheep had got stuck in the swamp.

But when Guillermo started toward the swamp, Mali raced ahead and showed him where Popo was lying beside the little tree. Then Guillermo picked him up in his arms and carried him back up the slope and laid him in the shade of a maguey. But Popo was a very big dog and was heavy to carry, and Guillermo was panting when he got him up the hill. Then Guillermo and Mali began to worry about how

they would get Popo home. And Popo worried, too, for it was certain he could not walk all that distance.

Suddenly Guillermo stood up and began to shout, and Mali and Oro both barked loudly. Popo raised his head to see what was the matter. And down on the long sunny road he saw Miguel and all the burros coming home from carrying loads to town. Miguel heard the shouting and stopped, and all the burros began to eat the sweet green grass that grew beside the long sunny road. And Guillermo picked Popo up and carried him down the hill to the road.

"Here, Salvador," shouted Miguel to one of the burros. "You are young and strong. You can carry Popo."

Then Popo realized that he must ride a burro home to the hacienda and he was terribly embarrassed. But there was no way out of it. If he could not walk he would have to ride. They hung him across Salvador's back and they all set out for home. Salvador was a friendly little burro, and he walked very carefully with Popo hanging across his back.

Suddenly Popo remembered another time he had ridden a burro. That was when he was a tiny puppy, and he had followed his mother when she set out with the sheep after staying home for a long time to take care of her puppies. Popo had gone along, and as today he had got very tired. And in the evening Celestino had come along with the burros, and they had laughed and put him on Chucha's back. But that time it was a joke and he was so little he sat straight up on Chucha's back and enjoyed it. That was when he and Chucha first became friends.

Now he looked around and there was the Oldest Burro walking beside him. She did not say anything, and Popo shut his eyes and pretended not to see her. He wanted only to get home now, and into his own shed to rest. He was ashamed that he could not do his work and had to ride home on Salvador's back.

The next day was Sunday. On that day no one worked on the hacienda, and all the burros were out in the meadow. When Popo took his walk that day and lay down to rest in the sun beside the maguey plant in the meadow, the Oldest Burro and Salvador came and asked him how he felt.

"I'm all right," said Popo. "I don't know what was the matter with me yesterday. Maybe it was something I had eaten."

"I'm sure of it," said Salvador. "There is a certain weed that grows among the sweet grass—"

"Foolish one," said the Oldest Burro, "dogs do not eat grass. Popo, you know perfectly well it was not something you ate. You know it is because you are too old to run after the sheep."

Popo sighed. It was useless to try to fool the Oldest Burro. She was too wise. "You are right, Chucha. I am old. I am of no use whatever to the human people who have cared for me for so many years."

"I am called Abuela now," said the Oldest Burro softly. "But when I was young I was called Chucha, and now only you remember it, Popo. Yes, we are getting old, you and I."

"But you are not so old," said Popo. "You still do your

work—you are strong and can run fast. And yet when I was a small puppy you were already a grown burro. How is that, Chucha?"

"It is only that burros have a longer life than dogs, just as men have a longer life than burros. You are lucky, Popo. Your time of work is finished now and you can rest."

"But I don't want to rest," said Popo. "I want to have a part in the work, so that I will still be important to the human people."

"But you still have a place to sleep," said old Chucha, "and they give you food to eat, don't they?"

"Yes," said Popo, "but I don't like being useless. I want the human people to say, 'Everything is safe because Popo is here.' I want to be important to them."

"Important!" snorted Chucha. "Of what use is importance? You are being foolish, Popo. I have no patience with foolishness."

And the Oldest Burro turned and walked away and began to eat the fresh green grass. Salvador looked after her and sniffed. He was used to the Oldest Burro and this habit of hers of walking away when anyone tried to discuss a problem that she thought was foolish. He felt very sorry for Popo. Popo sighed and stretched out in the sun.

"I'm sorry, Popo," said Salvador. "I am very stupid and cannot think of a way you can make yourself important to the human people. I don't even understand why you want to be important, so I am too stupid to help you. But if you want to go with the sheep every day, I will gladly carry you home when we come from town along the long sunny road."

"No," said Popo, "I know now I cannot go with the sheep. I shall have to think of something else. Go away now and let me sleep."

Salvador walked away—and he kept on walking. He went up the mountainside to the mountain meadow. And all the time he was feeling sorry for poor old Popo, and wondering why he wanted to be important. When he reached the brook that ran past the mountain meadow, Salvador met his friend, Raul the Coyote.

"Hello," said Raul, "why are you looking so sad today?"

"I am worried about Popo," said Salvador.

"Popo?" asked Raul. "I don't know Popo."

"He is the oldest dog at the hacienda," said Salvador. "And he is very unhappy because he is no longer important."

"I have heard of him from my mother," said Raul. "I believe he was once a very fierce dog, but I have not heard of him lately."

"That is because he is old now," said Salvador. "Listen, Raul, you are so wise, can you not think of a way to help him?"

"Why should I help him?" said Raul. "The dogs are my enemies. They are my cousins, but they are traitors to the animal people. They love only men. Now if the human people have turned against this Popo, he cannot expect the animal people to help him."

"They have not turned against him," said Salvador miserably. "It is just that he is so old he cannot run or guard the sheep, and he feels useless. I don't know what it means to be important, but that is what he wants. And you are so wise I thought you could help him."

Now Raul the Coyote is one of the wisest of the animals. He is very cunning and also has a sense of humor. So when Salvador told him about Popo he understood it, and he suddenly had an idea. He thought it a very good idea, and it amused him so much that he laughed out loud.

"All right, Salvador," said Raul, "I think I have an idea. After all, the dogs are cousins of the coyotes, and perhaps I should help him. Can you bring him to the bushes back of the low meadow to talk to me?"

"Oh yes," said Salvador. "He is sleeping in the meadow this minute. Come along."

"I'll meet you in the bushes behind the meadow," said Raul. "I prefer going the longer way and keeping in the shadow. You run across the meadow and fetch your Popo."

So Salvador raced back down the mountainside and went to where Popo was still sleeping in the sun. He woke him up and told him that Raul the Coyote had a fine idea, and could tell him how to make himself important to the human people.

"Raul the Coyote?" said Popo. "But the coyotes are enemies of the hacienda. How can I be friends with a coyote?"

"But Raul says they are your cousins," said Salvador. "He says when you are old you are no longer enemies. And since you are cousins he will help you."

"Well," said Popo, "we shall see what he has to say."

Popo got up stiffly and went with Salvador down across

the meadow to the bushes on the other side of the valley. And there was Raul waiting for him.

"Here we are," said Salvador happily.

"How are your teeth, Friend of Man?" said Raul.

"Teeth?" said Popo. "Once I sharpened them on the hides of coyotes." Then he added bitterly, "But now they are worn down to the gums. I eat gruel now. Think of it! Gruel and ground meat!"

Raul laughed. "Yes, you are old," he said. "And even though you are a friend of the human people you are, after all, my cousin, and too old to be an enemy. So I will help you. Does it ever happen that all the other dogs are away from the hacienda?"

"Sometimes," said Popo cautiously. "Why do you ask?"

"You want the human people to think you are still of great use to them," said Raul, "and I will tell you a way. Here is the plan. You must tell me when all the other dogs are to be away, for naturally I do not want to risk my own life to help you. But on a night when you are the only dog at the hacienda I will come, and you will be watching for me. I will steal the biggest turkey from the pen. I must really grab the turkey so that he will set up a loud noise and bring the people out to watch your triumph. Then when the turkey yells, you will come dashing out and grab my tail—even now I would rather have you grab my tail than my throat—and I will drop the turkey and run. Then the people will praise you for being a fine watch dog, and will give you credit for driving me away and saving the turkey."

As Raul talked Popo could imagine it all. He could see the people running out from the house and seeing him fight with the coyote. No one would expect him to kill the coyote, because he had no teeth. But he would save the turkey and chase the coyote away. And the people would praise him and would know that he was still a fine watch dog. It was a marvelous idea.

"That is a good idea," said Popo, "and I will be very grateful to you for helping me. As it happens, we can do it this very night. There is a tiger in the mountains that has been killing the colts in the high pasture; and last night the men went out with all the dogs to catch him. But they did not get him, and they are going out again tonight. They will go as soon as it is dark."

"Fine. I'll be there two hours after dark. And remember, you are to grab only my tail."

Raul suddenly disappeared in the bushes, and Salvador and Popo went back across the meadow. They were both happy and were sure this was going to make everything all right for Popo.

That night Popo lay on his bed in the shed and waited for Raul. It seemed a long time, and Popo was excited, thinking about what a hero he was going to be and how the family would praise him. Then he got the scent of the coyote on the wind. But he lay still and waited. Raul had said the turkey would make a noise. Pretty soon Popo heard the commotion in the turkey pen, and then a great squawking.

He jumped up and ran out to the pen, barking as loud as

he could. And there was Raul just jumping over the fence
with the biggest turkey in his mouth. And the turkey was
squawking at the top of his voice. Just then the door opened
and all the family came running out. Popo dashed after Raul
and grabbed his tail.

"Drop him now! Drop him and run!" cried Popo with his
mouth full of bushy tail.

Raul laughed, a cunning little laugh. "I'll run all right,"
said Raul, and his voice was muffled, too, for his mouth was
filled with the turkey that he was still holding. "I'll run now,
but I have changed my mind about dropping him, you foolish
old dog."

Then Raul jerked his tail out of Popo's mouth and dashed
away in the darkness. The turkey had stopped squawking because he was dead now. But he was still in Raul's mouth.

Popo was so surprised that for a moment he just stood
there. He could hear the family shouting and saying, "Good
old Popo."

Then suddenly he was very angry with Raul and dashed
after him. But Popo could not run very fast because he was so
old. And Raul was already so far away that he could not even
get his scent on the wind. So Popo turned and limped back.

All the family was still out by the corrals, and they had a
lantern. When Popo came back they all petted him and
praised him for being brave.

"Good old Popo," they said. "Of course he could not kill
the coyote because he is too old, and he has no teeth. But he
was not afraid to try. The coyote got away with the biggest

turkey, but at least Popo did his best to protect the hacienda."

Poor old Popo was so ashamed of himself that he could not even wag his tail.

"It worked all right," thought Popo. "The family is praising me. But me—I feel worse than ever. For the turkey is dead, and it is my fault. The coyote would not have come tonight if I had not told him the young dogs would be gone."

He managed an apologetic wag and went back to his place in the shed. "It just goes to show," he thought, "that people never change much. A coyote is always a coyote, no matter what promises he makes."

How Papantla Got Its Patron Saint

FOUR HUNDRED years ago in the hot country of Mexico, a straight young tree grew on the very edge of the jungle. There were many animals in the jungle country, and all of them were friends of the straight young tree. Now you understand that trees cannot run about making new friends the way animals and people do, so they become very fond of the friends who come to them.

150

All the people in that part of the country were Totonaca Indians. They were dark, laughing people who loved fiestas and visiting. The straight young tree loved the people, but there was one thing about them that distressed her very much. That was their religion.

You see, four hundred years ago the Indians who lived in Mexico had not heard about God and Jesus and the Virgin Mary. They worshipped strange gods of whom they made stone idols. One of their idols was on a huge shrine just at the edge of the jungle, right beside the straight young tree. And in the village of Papantla, which the little tree could see quite clearly in the nearby hills, there were many more idols.

But it was not the idols that distressed the lovely tree. It was a queer habit the Totonaca had of offering them sacrifices of animals. They were always coming into the jungle, and catching the animal friends of the lovely tree and killing them to give as offerings to the idols. The young tree would rustle her leaves and sigh, and try to tell the people this was wrong. But it is difficult for a tree to make human people understand.

Then one day the Franciscan priests came from across the sea. They came to Papantla and to all the villages of the Totonaca to teach them the beliefs of the Christians.

The Totonaca thought the new religion was a good one, and they liked the beautiful churches the priests built. But they kept right on making sacrifices to their old gods, and were not so much interested in God and Jesus and Mary as the priests wanted them to be. The lovely young tree heard the priests explain to the people of Papantla that they should make a beautiful image of the Virgin Mary, and put it in their church as their patron saint. Then the Virgin herself would come into the church and help them learn to be good Christians.

The people of Papantla nodded their heads and agreed that this was a fine idea. Then they went off and made a fiesta in the new church. But they did nothing about the image of the Virgin.

The little tree worried about it. She asked the animal people of the jungle if any of the Totonaca were doing anything about new images for the beautiful new churches.

"Oh, yes," said the tiger. "The jungle is scarcely safe these days. The people of all the villages—except Papantla—are coming into the forest hunting fine straight trees from which to make images."

Mazaquate, the Boa Constrictor, slid around a bamboo thicket and looked at the straight young tree.

"As a matter of fact," said Mazaquate, "you are exactly the kind of tree they look for. Shouldn't be surprised if they would cut you down and carve a saint from your strong straight trunk."

The young tree shivered. Then suddenly she was very happy. She shook her leaves and lifted her head. Away on the nearby hill she could see the shimmering rosy glow of the new stone church of Papantla.

"I should like that," she said. "I love the people of Papantla. I should like being an image of the Virgin in their church."

"Some people have queer ideas," said Mazaquate, and he slithered away into the bamboo thicket.

"Very queer, indeed," said the tiger. "I've seen too many of our animal friends sacrificed, to want anything to do with any religion."

"But don't you see," said the little tree quickly, "this religion is different? That is why I want to help with it—so there will be no more sacrifices."

The tiger just looked at her and shook his head.

"Some people will believe anything," he said. "But you will not be in the church of Papantla. Of all the villages of the Totonaca, only Papantla is doing nothing about the images for the new church." And the tiger got up and stalked off into the jungle.

The straight young tree looked away to the village of Papantla and wondered what the inside of the church looked like. And she wondered how it would feel to be cut loose from her roots and made into a saint.

The next morning very early, just as the first rays of the sun fell across the jungle and began to lift the deep shadows of the woods, the little tree woke up and began to think again about being an image of the Virgin. She looked at the soft blue of the early morning sky, and suddenly she knew exactly what she would look like when she was made into an image of the Virgin Mary. She could see Mary quite plainly, standing there beside her at the edge of the jungle. Her face was dark like the Indians. She wore a wide blue skirt, the color of the morning sky. And on her head was a crown of jungle flowers, and about her shoulders a white lacy quexquen (which is the Totonaca word for a small shawl such as the Totonaca women wear).

Just then the young tree heard the tramp of men's feet along the jungle path. She could still see the shimmering vision of the Virgin beside her. Then as the men came nearer, the vision disappeared and there was only the gleam of the early sun on the jungle flowers. The men had stopped and were staring toward the young tree.

"Did you see that?" said one of the men. "I saw the Virgin, in a full blue skirt, standing beside that tree."

"I saw her, too," said another, "but she is gone now."

"It was a sign to us," another one said. "We must cut down that very tree and take it back to Tecolutla, and use it to make an image of the Virgin for our patron saint."

"We will make it like the vision we saw," they all cried at once, "with a wide blue skirt and a white quexquen and a crown of jungle flowers. And we will call her the Blue Virgin of Tecolutla."

"Look," said the first man. "We are very close to Papantla. The people of Papantla may object to our cutting a tree so close to their village."

"It doesn't matter," said the others all at once. "It is the free forest. Besides, we saw the Virgin beside that tree, and for that reason we must have that very tree to make the image for our church in Tecolutla."

So all the men gathered around the little tree, and lifted their machetes and began to cut her down. The little tree was frightened. These were not the people of Papantla. They came from Tecolutla, and they would take her away to their own village.

As the machetes cut into her trunk, she rustled her leaves and groaned and cried out to them.

"Don't cut me down!" she cried. "I belong to Papantla! The Virgin you saw came to be the patron saint of Papantla! You must not take me away from Papantla!"

But the men of Tecolutla heard only the rustling of the leaves, and the creaking of the tree as their machetes cut into it. They could not understand what the little tree was saying. So they cut her down, and lopped off her branches, and dragged the straight strong trunk of the tree away with them to the village of Tecolutla.

Then the wood carvers went to work, and from the fine dark wood of the tree they carved a beautiful image of the Virgin Mary. They carved her with a wide full skirt, which they painted the soft blue of the morning sky. They gave her a white quexquen, and on her head they put a crown of jungle flowers. Then they put her into the church of Tecolutla, and called her the Blue Virgin of Tecolutla. And they brought her offerings of fruits and flowers.

But the heart of the straight young tree, that was now an image of the Virgin, was still thinking about Papantla. She still felt that she belonged to the people of Papantla, and that she should be standing in their church.

So that night, very late, when all the candles were blown out and all the people had gone home to bed, the new Blue

Virgin stepped down from her pedestal and walked out through the sleeping village. She went along the jungle path, past the dead stump where she had grown as a tree, past the huge shrine of the old stone idol, and straight on into the village of Papantla.

She walked into the church of rosy stone and looked around. There in the front of the church, above the altar, was the great niche where the priests had told the people of Papantla they should put an image of the Virgin. But of course the niche was empty, because the people of Papantla had never bothered to carve an image to put into it.

The new Blue Virgin walked through the air, straight into the niche. Her dark Indian face smiled into the darkness of the church, and her small brown hands held her gold cross above the altar. This was where she belonged.

In the morning the people of Papantla were amazed when they saw the lovely Virgin in their church. The first people who saw her ran about telling all the other people. And very soon the whole village came to look at her.

"What a miracle!" they cried. "We did nothing about an image for our church, but here one has come to us all by herself! Truly the people of Papantla are lucky!"

"Think of it!" said others. "Although we do no carving, our patron saint appears in our church! We shall call her the Virgin of Papantla, because she chose us herself!"

For a week no one could talk of anything else. Even the people in other villages heard about the miraculous new Virgin of Papantla.

And after a few days the people of Tecolutla heard about it. They had been hunting everywhere for their lost Blue Virgin, and now they heard that Papantla had a new Virgin with a wide blue skirt and a crown of jungle flowers.

Of course, the people of Tecolutla went straight to Papantla and demanded to see the Virgin.

"But that is our Blue Virgin," they cried. "You have stolen her from our church, and now we are going to take her home with us."

"We did not steal her," said the people of Papantla. "She came to us of her own accord."

The priests and the Chief of Papantla made inquiries, but no one had been to Tecolutla. Nevertheless, everyone knew that the wood carvers of Tecolutla had carved a Virgin, and all the people of Tecolutla swore this was the one.

"What can we do?" said the people of Papantla.

They shrugged their shoulders, and gave the Virgin back to the people of Tecolutla.

So the Virgin of Papantla was carried back along the jungle path, out past the huge shrine of the old stone idol, past the dead stump where she had grown as a tree, and back to the church of Tecolutla. She was very unhappy because she wanted to stay in Papantla.

That night the Chief of Tecolutla put men on guard at the church, so that no one could come and steal the Blue Virgin. But when all the candles were blown out, and all the village was asleep, and the guards were drowsing by the door of the church, the Blue Virgin came down from her pedestal and walked out through the sleeping village.

She went back along the jungle path, past the dead stump where she had grown as a tree, past the huge shrine of the old stone idol, and right into the rosy stone church of Papantla. And in the morning when the people of Papantla went to church, there was the Virgin of Papantla, smiling at them with her dark Indian face.

Now when the people of Tecolutla saw that again their Virgin was gone, they went straight to Papantla. And sure enough, there she was. They were very angry now, and they threatened to make a war against Papantla if they did not stop stealing their Blue Virgin.

"We did not steal her," they answered. "She came to us of her own accord. But you may take her away again."

They were sad to lose the lovely miraculous Virgin, but they shrugged their shoulders and gave her back to the people of Tecolutla.

That night the Chief of Tecolutla put a guard of many men about the church. They stood all night with their machetes in their hands, watching the church to see that no one entered and stole the Blue Virgin. But when all the candles were blown out and the church was in darkness, the Blue Virgin walked out through the air over the heads of the guards. And no one saw her go. In the morning she was back again in the church of Papantla.

Now this time the people of Tecolutla were very, very angry. The whole village went to Papantla, and they told the Chief of Papantla that unless he caught the thief who was stealing their Virgin, they would certainly make a great war against them. And they would destroy all their crops and their houses, and even the new church of rosy stone.

By this time the people of Papantla were worried, too. So that night the Chief of Papantla set a strong guard all around the church, to keep watch and see if they could catch the thief when he came carrying the Virgin to their church.

And the Chief of Tecolutla set a stronger guard than ever around their church. All the men of the village were there. They stood one against the other all the way around the church, so that no one could possibly pass between them and get into the church to steal the lovely Blue Virgin. They even left the candles in the church burning all night.

But toward morning, as the candles burned low, the Blue Virgin stepped off her pedestal and walked out through the air above the heads of the guards. And none of them saw her go.

The next morning the Chief of Papantla went to the church and asked the guards if anyone had come in the night, carrying the Virgin of Papantla. They told him that all night they had watched without once falling asleep, and no one had entered the church. Then they went inside, and there, in the big niche over the altar, the Virgin of Papantla was smiling at them with her dark Indian face.

Then the Chief of Papantla and all his men started out to Tecolutla. Beside the huge shrine of the old stone idol they met the Chief of Tecolutla and all his men, going to Papantla.

"The Virgin is back in the church of Papantla," said the

Chief of Papantla, "but all these men who were on guard at the church will swear that no one entered the church in the night."

"We know that she is gone from our church," said the Chief of Tecolutla, "and yet all these men who were on guard will swear that no one entered the church to steal her."

All the guards of both villages swore that was true. So they all agreed that it must indeed be a miracle, and that it would do no good to fight a war about it.

"But the fact remains," said the Chief of Tecolutla, "that our wood carvers made the image that now stands in your church."

"That is true," said the Chief of Papantla. "But it is clear that the Virgin wants to stay with us. Suppose we give you twenty measures of corn to pay for the work your wood carvers did for us."

"Give us the twenty measures of corn," said the Chief of Tecolutla, "and add to that thirty turkeys. For remember we are giving you also the vision which we saw. And you must see that now our wood carvers must make another image for our own church, without a vision to go by."

"That is fair," said the Chief of Papantla. "We were lazy about carving an image. And we did not even get out to see the vision of our patron saint. But when we get both the saint and the image in spite of that we do not mind paying for it."

He sent some of his men back to Papantla to get the twenty measures of corn and the thirty turkeys for the men of Tecolutla. Then everybody heaved a great sigh of relief because there was to be no war.

At that moment the captain of the Papantla guards looked at the huge shrine of the old stone idol. It reminded him that they had all been forgetting about the idol during these days of excitement over the new Virgin.

"That reminds me," he said. "We have not made an offering to our idol for a long time. He may be angry."

"Oh, no!" said the Chief of Papantla. "You remember the priests said that the Virgin Mary does not approve of the old idols, and she especially does not approve of sacrificing animals. Now that she has performed a miracle and sent a miraculous image to be our patron saint, we must never again kill an animal for sacrifice."

So the men of Papantla toppled the stone idol off his shrine, and rolled him into the jungle. No one noticed the dead stump where the Virgin of Papantla had once grown as a straight young tree. But they all went home and made a fiesta in her honor.

All this happened more than three hundred years ago, but the lovely Virgin of Papantla still stands in the niche above the altar in the rosy stone church of Papantla. If you ever go there you can see her for yourself, smiling with her dark Indian face. And you will see that she still wears her wide skirt of the soft blue of the morning sky, and her white quexquen, and a crown of jungle flowers. And all the animals of the jungle are safe from sacrifice.

The River That Was Stolen

IN MEXICO they say that long ago on the warm western
slope of the low mountains in the land where the Tarascans
live, the river Cupatitzio flowed through the town of Uruapan. For that reason, all the animal people and all the human
people who lived in Uruapan considered themselves very
lucky. For you must know that every animal and every growing thing needs water in order to live.

162

So it was that Uruapan was a happy village. The river came down from the high mountains into the low mountains, and flowed gently through the village. Then it plunged over the edge of the hills, down into the hot country, and on to the great sea. It was not a big river, but in the village of Uruapan it was wide and beautiful. And along its banks the great trees were heavy with fruit and flowers, and the fields bore so much grain that the animal people came in from the forest to share it with the human people. And there was plenty for all.

The only trouble was that Uruapan had to be a very small village, for the river was wide and beautiful only in that one small valley. And to enjoy the water, the village huddled close to its banks and did not spread out much. Just the same, everyone was happy, for other villages in the low mountains had very little water, and it was difficult for them to raise enough fruit and grain to feed themselves.

Now it happened that about that time, which was more than four hundred years ago, the Franciscan Friars came across the ocean from Spain. They traveled all over the land of Mexico, teaching the Indians the religion of the Christians. They went to all the villages of the Tarascans. And of course, they went to Uruapan on the banks of the lovely Cupatitzio.

Before that the Tarascans had worshipped strange gods. And in all their villages they had great fierce-looking stone idols, representing their gods. And every day they made offerings of animals to them. But when the Franciscans came and told them about God and Jesus and Mary, they liked the new religion. And they tumbled the idols off their shrines and rolled them into the Cupatitzio.

Then they helped the friars build a neat little church in the plaza. And the trees had more fruit than ever and everyone was very happy.

Then a terrible thing happened.

One morning when the people got up and went out to work in their fields, there was no water in the Cupatitzio. No one did any work that day, because everyone was running around talking about the river and wondering what had become of all the water.

They thought that surely the water would soon come down from the mountains again. But the whole day passed and the water did not come—then another day, and another. The ground that had been the bottom of the river dried in the sun, and there was nothing but dust in the once lovely Cupatitzio. And in the dust lay the fierce stone idols that the people had thrown into the river.

When three days had passed the men of the village set out to look for the river. They walked up the side of the mountain where the Cupatitzio should have been, but there was not a sign of the river. At last on the mountainside high above the town, the little path and even the bed of the river disappeared. In their places rose a sheer, black hill.

"Look," said the Chief of Uruapan. "I have never seen that hill before. Surely this is where the Cupatitzio has always flowed, and now we find this great black hill! Has anyone ever seen this hill before?"

Everyone answered at once:

"I have never seen it before!"

"Nor I!"

"It has never been here before!"

"Certainly this hill was not here when we came this way hunting last week. We could not be mistaken. Last week the Cupatitzio was here."

"It is very puzzling," said the Chief. "We must climb over the new mountain and see if we can find the Cupatitzio."

But when they tried to climb the strange new mountain they found it quite impossible. Nothing grew on the black hill. Not a tree, nor a bush, nor a blade of grass. There was nothing to hold to with their hands. And the side of the hill was so steep and smooth there was no place to set their feet. Moreover, the rock of the new black hill was so hot that it burned their hands when they touched it.

"It is very puzzling," said the Chief. "But if we cannot climb it, we will go around it. We must find our river."

So they set out to walk around the hill. The sun was hot and the sleek black hill reflected the sun and made it even hotter. At last they went around the end of the hill and walked along the upper side toward the place where the Cupatitzio should come down from the high mountains.

As they walked they noticed that there were no animals at all on the paths near the mountain.

"It is very puzzling," said the Chief. "There are always many animals in this part of the woods, yet today we see none."

At last they came to the place where the Cupatitzio should come down from the hills. But there was nothing but a great heap of boulders. Under the rocks they could hear the moaning of the river, but they could not see the water.

"It is very puzzling," said the Chief. "We must climb up over the boulders and see if we can find the Cupatitzio higher up the mountain. We must find our river."

So they climbed over the boulders and on up the side of the mountain. And there on the other side of the heap of boulders they found the small upper end of the Cupatitzio. It was still coming down from the high mountain, and trying its best to get to Uruapan. But at the heap of boulders above the strange new hill, the poor little river disappeared into the ground, and that seemed to be the end of it.

While the men of Uruapan stood beside the little stream and wondered where it had gone, down under the boulders and the new black hill, two deer came out of the woods. They stood staring toward the black hill and then toward the cool water. Anyone could see they were very thirsty. But as they looked at the black mountain they suddenly began to tremble. Then they turned and dashed away into the woods again.

"It is very puzzling," said the Chief. "Even the animals will not come to the Cupatitzio to drink when they see the black mountain. I do believe they are afraid of it."

"Perhaps the mountain is bewitched," someone said.

"They say," said another, "that the animals always know when a thing is bewitched. They can smell the witches and are afraid of them."

"It is very puzzling," said the Chief. "Since none of us has ever seen that mountain before, and since it certainly has swallowed our Cupatitzio, I should think that it was put there by the witches, except for one thing. The priests of our new religion tell us there are no witches. They say there are only God and Jesus and their saints. So how could the witches make a mountain if there are no witches?"

Then one of the men, who was very old and still loved the old gods, walked up to the Chief and spoke in a low voice.

"Perhaps that is the trouble, my son," he whispered. "Perhaps the priests are wrong. For many years our people have believed in the old gods. Now we have deserted them and thrown their idols into the Cupatitzio. And see what happens! A strange new hill arises on the mountainside to swallow the Cupatitzio. Our fields are drying in the sun and we shall all die if we do not get the water into the village again. Perhaps the old gods have sent the witches to steal the water, so that their idols, that we threw into the river, are uncovered before our eyes."

"It is very puzzling," said the Chief. "The new religion seems good, and yet our river has been stolen. It certainly looks as though the old gods might be angry with us."

"There is only one thing to do," insisted the old man. "We must go home and set up the idols again, and make offerings to them. Then perhaps they will remove the new black mountain and give us back our river."

All the men of Uruapan walked back around the hot black mountain, and down the dusty path to the village. When they reached the village all the women and children were waiting for them. They began shouting to the men as they approached:

"Did you find the river?"

"What has become of the Cupatitzio?"

"How will we live if we do not have our river?"

"It is very puzzling," said the Chief. "A great, hot, black hill has risen on the mountainside to swallow the Cupatitzio. The old gods must be angry. We must set up the idols again and make offerings at once."

All the village was very sad, for they liked the new church and the kind God the Franciscans had brought them. But after all, what could they do? They would die if they did not get their river back again.

So they hurried to the place where the river once had been, and lifted up the fierce stone idols and set them on the altars again. Then they went into the woods to catch some animals and kill them for offerings to the old gods.

Now the animal people of the forest had been very happy since the Tarascans had the Christian religion, for that meant that none of them was sacrificed to the old gods any more. Of course, the people still came hunting some of them to eat. But they killed only a few that way, and the animals were used to it. They were philosophical about being killed for food. That was the law of the forest and they could understand it. But they did not like the sacrifices that took so many of their lives and did no one any good.

Since the Franciscans came there had been no sacrifices and the animals were happy. Now again the Tarascans came catching animals for sacrifice, and there was consternation in the forest. This was even worse than that horrible, unnatural hill that had suddenly appeared on the mountain to swallow the beautiful river.

The next morning at dawn all the village was gathered at the shrine of the biggest idol. They had caught four deer, and many rabbits and quails and squirrels, and had even a frightened little tlacuache and many bright-plumaged birds. The old man, who had been a priest of the old gods before the Franciscans came, was ready with knives and fire. And when the sun came up he would sacrifice the animals and birds.

But just as the sun sent his first rays over the top of the eastern mountains, someone came out of the house of the Franciscans and started through the streets toward the church. It was a tall, kind-faced priest, called Juan de San Miguel.

Father Juan saw all the people gathered about the old shrine. Then he saw the fierce, stone idol back in his place, and the fire ready on the altar.

"What is this?" said Father Juan. "What are you doing?"

"As you see," said the old man, "we are about to make sacrifices to our old gods, so that they will give us back our river."

"It is very puzzling, Padre," said the Chief. "We do not

like to desert the new religion, but the mountain is bewitched
and a strange black hill has risen on the mountainside to
swallow the Cupatitzio. You must know we will all die if
we do not have water."

"It is not so puzzling," said Father Juan. "Do you not
know that the Devil always tries to make life hard for people
who want to be good Christians? It is only necessary to recog-
nize him, and to convince him that he cannot hurt you. Free
the animals, and come and show me this bewitched mountain."

The people knew that Father Juan loved them and wanted
to help them. But they were not quite sure he could do it
this time. Nevertheless, they did not know how to refuse to
go with him and show him the new mountain. They whispered among themselves and decided they must go. But they
did not free the animals. They shut them up in pens and boxes
so they could sacrifice them later, after they had shown the
mountain to Father Juan.

Father Juan and all the people of Uruapan walked up
the path beside the dusty river bed where the Cupatitzio had
once flowed, until they came to the strange black mountain.

"It is very puzzling," said the Chief. "Last week the Cupatitzio came this way down the mountainside to our town.
But now you can see for yourself, here is a hot, black hill that
no one has ever seen before."

"It is not so puzzling," said Father Juan. "Can you not
see, that is not a real mountain, but the Devil himself? See how
smooth and hot are the black sides. And nothing grows on

the hill—not a tree, nor a bush, nor a blade of grass."

Then Father Juan lifted his hands and shouted as loud as he could.

"What are you doing here, Devil? We want our river back again."

The black hill rumbled a little but only settled deeper into the side of the mountain. The people were afraid now, and they fell back into a half circle, spreading out on the two sides of the river bed where the Cupatitzio had once flowed below the black hill. Then all the animal people of the woods arrived to see what was happening. The animal people made another half circle behind the human people, and they all waited to see what would happen next.

Then the good Father Juan walked boldly up to the black hill and laid his hand on its hot smooth side.

"Begone, Devil, in the name of God!" cried Father Juan.

For you must know that, although the Devil may be very powerful, it is impossible for him to disobey when a believer says, "In the name of God."

So now the great black hill trembled and shook, and rose a little higher into the air. But it was still there. Once more Father Juan shouted at it:

"In the name of God, begone! Give us back our river!"

This time the hill rose until it was a great black figure, as big as the mountain. And he shook and rumbled, and the boulders rolled down the mountainside. But he still knelt with one knee in the earth, holding the place where the Cupatitzio had been swallowed. So for a third time Father Juan shouted:

"Begone, Devil, in the name of God! Give us back the beautiful Cupatitzio!"

And this time it worked. There was a great groaning from above the trees, and the boulders rattled down the side of the mountain. With a noise like thunder, a great cloud of smoke rose from the place where the black hill had been. The last part of him they could see was the great black knee planted deep in the soft earth. Then that, too, was gone, and for a moment everyone saw the mark of the huge knee. And not a boulder rolled into that big hole, although they rolled on both sides of it down the mountainside.

Then the Cupatitzio rushed up from the depths of the earth where it had been buried, and plunged down among the boulders to fill the huge pool left by the Devil's knee. Everyone shouted for joy. When the pool was filled the water rushed out into the dusty river bed and on down the mountain, where it had always flowed.

But the Cupatitzio was so glad to be coming back to the Tarascans that it was not content to fill one river. The pool overflowed, and the boulders helped the water to cut a new channel. And there, before the eyes of everyone, a new river went plunging down the side of the mountain.

All the animal people, and all the human people, shouted for joy. And everyone crowded round to look into the blue depths of the new pool. They crowded so close that the old man slipped and fell into the clear cold water. Everyone was frightened because the old man could not swim. But he climbed out quite unhurt before anyone could help him.

"Well," said the old man, "at least I was the first in the water of the new pool given us by the goodness of God. With such a deity how can anyone think of sacrificing animals to the old gods?" He looked around him fiercely. "Go home at once and free the animals."

"Well, bless my soul!" said the Chief. "It is a magic pool! It has cured the old man of his devotion to the old gods. Let us all go home and free the animals."

Everyone went back down the mountainside between the two rivers—the old Cupatitzio and the new river that was cutting its channel carefully among the houses on the other side of the village.

"It is very puzzling," said the Chief. "They tell us there are no witches. Then a witch comes and swallows the Cupatitzio. For centuries the Cupatitzio has been a single river, and now, having been bewitched, it comes back to us twins. And it brings us, besides, a magic pool."

"It is very puzzling, indeed," said the old man. "But do not question it. Now we have two Cupatitzios. Let it go at that. With so much water we can enlarge our village and fields to fill the whole valley."

Now all this happened four hundred years ago, and the priests in the church will not swear that it is true, so I cannot swear either. But it is the story the Tarascans tell.

It is certainly true that Uruapan is still there in the western mountains, and that two beautiful rivers flow through the town. And anyone will show you the Pool of the Devil's

Knee, that is exactly the right shape, with not a single boulder in the pool, although there are hundreds of boulders around its edge.

The Tarascans will tell you, too, that the pool is still magic, for anyone who bathes in its clean blue water cannot help believing in the goodness of God.

And certain it is that there are no stone idols in the village of Uruapan, and all the animal people are safe from sacrifice.

Sarita and the Duendes

IN MEXICO they say that the woodlands are peopled with duendes, and these queer little folks often come into the towns to play jokes on the human people.

Of course, most people cannot see the duendes, so they do not believe in them. That seems foolish, because we cannot see the wind either, and yet we all believe in the wind. But there are people all over the world who do believe

175

in the duendes. There are different names for them in different countries. In countries where Spanish is spoken, as in
Mexico, they call them duendes. In Ireland they call them
leprechauns, and in America and England they call them
elves.

Well, this is the story of a little duende named Donato.
He was very small—just about twelve inches tall—and he
looked like a tiny little old man. That is an odd thing about
duendes. They are all little old men—never girl duendes and
never baby duendes. But in spite of looking like little old men,
the duendes are never old, no matter how many years they
live.

So Donato and his twelve brothers were just like naughty
small boys. They lived in a beautiful grove close to a pretty
town called Cuautla. To amuse themselves they often went
into Cuautla where they opened the pens and let the chickens
out, and teased the dogs and made them bark, and went into
children's rooms and turned on the electric lights, and hid
their hats and school books, so their mothers scolded them
for carelessness. Donato and all his brothers were very mischievous, but at times they were very kind.

One day they were running through the woods, when they
heard someone crying. And there, under a tree, lay a little
boy, weeping as though his heart were breaking.

"Hello," said Donato, "why are you making so much
noise?"

The little boy sat up and looked around him. But there
was no one in sight.

"Where are you?" asked the boy, "and who are you?"

Donato laughed. "I am Donato. And I know you. Your name is Lorenzo."

"Yes," said Lorenzo. "But where are you?"

The voice seemed very close, but there was nothing to be seen but a little rock. Lorenzo stared at the rock. And, suddenly, there was Donato, sitting on the rock with his legs crossed, and laughing at him.

"Caramba!" said Lorenzo. "You are a duende!"

"You are a bright boy to guess that," chuckled Donato. "And now will you tell me why you were crying? Really that was an awful noise. It is much easier to laugh, and it sounds better."

"Oh," Lorenzo puckered up his face and Donato was afraid he was going to cry again. But he didn't—not very much, anyway. "Well," he said, "it is about my mother. I don't believe she loves me—not the way other boys' mothers love them."

"Let me see," said Donato, wrinkling up his eyes to think. "Your mother's name is Sarita, isn't it?"

"Yes," said Lorenzo, "how did you know?"

"We duendes know everyone," said Donato. "We should. We've been playing jokes on the people of Cuautla for more than a hundred years. Now this Sarita—she is very lazy. She always was, even when she was a little girl. But I did think she loved her little boy. What makes you think she doesn't love you?"

"Well, for one thing," said Lorenzo, "she won't mend my

clothes, and when I go to school the other children laugh at me. And almost every day when I come home from school she has forgotten to cook dinner. So I have to eat just tortillas, or else wait until she cooks dinner. Then I'm late for school and the teacher scolds me."

"Hmmmmm!" said Donato. "What else does she do?"

"Well," said Lorenzo, "I am always ashamed."

"Ashamed? What are you ashamed of?"

"Because my mother never cleans the house. It is always very dirty, and I am ashamed for the other children to come to see me, because all of them live in clean houses."

"Hmmmm!" said Donato. "That still doesn't prove she doesn't love you. What else does she do?"

"Well," said Lorenzo, "she and my father quarrel a great deal, and that makes me unhappy."

"Why do they quarrel?"

"My father gets cross because the house is dirty and she forgets to cook dinner in time for him to eat when he comes home from work. And when they quarrel they both forget all about me."

"Hmmmm! Hmmmm!" said Donato. Then he threw his head back and laughed so loud that all his twelve brothers came running to get in on the fun. And they looked so funny —all the little duendes, with their wrinkled old faces and gay green caps, that Lorenzo laughed, too.

"Well, Lorenzo, well, well," said Donato. "There's nothing wrong with your mother except that she is very lazy. But I can see that this makes it hard on you. What do you say,

Brothers, shall we help Lorenzo? Shall we give him the kind of mother he likes?"

"Oh, I love my mother," said Lorenzo quickly. "It is just that I want her to love me, too—and—and—and patch my pants for me."

"Of course, of course," chuckled Donato. "Well, Brothers, what do you say? Shall we cure Sarita?"

"Sure, it will be fun!" shouted all the brother duendes.

"Then stop worrying, Lorenzo," said Donato. "We'll take good care of everything, because you are a good boy and you are very truthful. But, for mercy's sake, don't weep in our woods any more. It sounds terrible."

Lorenzo did not want to talk any more about the awful noise he made weeping, so he said: "How do you know I am truthful?"

"Because," said Donato softly, "if you were not a good, truthful little boy, with imagination and understanding, you would not be able to see us."

"Well, thank you—" Lorenzo began.

Then he stopped suddenly and stared around him, in surprise. For there was not a duende in sight! But there was a great shout of duende laughter that rippled away through the woods and changed into the sound of the wind, blowing through the trees. Then Lorenzo got up and went home.

The next morning when Lorenzo awoke the sun was shining through the window and his room was just as untidy as usual. He thought about his conversation with the duendes, but it did not seem very real this morning. So he was sure he must have dreamed it. His mother did not really love him. Yes, certainly, it was only a dream about the duendes.

He got up and put on his pair of pants which was torn only a little down each leg. The other pair had most of the seat torn out of it. He heard his father, whose name was Juan, cooking breakfast in the kitchen. Lorenzo went into the kitchen.

"Papá, I dreamed about the duendes last night. Do you think there really are duendes?"

"Of course not," said Juan. "Here, take this ten centavos and run down to the bakery and get some buns. Your mother never has anything in the house to eat. Duendes, indeed! We ought to have some duendes around here to do the work!"

Lorenzo took the ten centavos and went out into the street. His father was most unreasonable. How could he expect duendes to do the work if there weren't any duendes? He thought he saw a flash of green—like the funny green caps the duendes wore—outside his mother's window. But that was probably just his imagination, because of the dream he had about the duendes. So he went on down the street.

But it wasn't his imagination. For just at that moment Donato and all twelve of his brothers jumped through the window into Sarita's room. Sarita was asleep in her bed, but even if she were awake Donato knew that she could not see them. Then you should have seen what those duendes did!

Donato pulled the covers off of Sarita, and one of his brothers tickled her in the ribs and woke her up. Another one grabbed her feet and pulled them off the edge of the bed. So the first thing she knew, Sarita was up and standing on the floor. She yawned sleepily and started to sit down again. But Donato poked her in the back, and she looked around—surprised and wide awake now. But she could not see a thing.

"That's funny," said Sarita. "I always like to sleep late. I wonder why I woke up so early and feel like getting up. Well, I'll just go out and see if Juan has some coffee made, then I'll go back to bed."

But Donato put her dress in her hand, and one of his duende brothers set her shoes under her feet, and another brother yanked her night dress off. So before she knew it Sarita was getting dressed. When she was dressed she walked out to the kitchen, still thinking about getting herself a cup of coffee.

But in the kitchen Donato suddenly thrust a skillet into her hand, and one of his brothers seized the dish of eggs and put it into her other hand. Juan looked up from his coffee and saw her, with the eggs and the skillet, standing by the stove.

"Why, Sarita!" cried Juan. "You did get up! And you are going to scramble me some eggs! How sweet of you! And I was just sitting here being angry with you because there are no buns for breakfast."

Juan got up and went and kissed Sarita. She was so surprised she could not say a thing. She did not know how she happened to have the skillet and the eggs in her hands. But now that Juan was so pleased, there was nothing for her to do but go ahead and scramble some eggs for breakfast. So when Lorenzo came home with the buns, there was his mother sitting at the table all dressed and smiling, and his father beside her pleased and happy. And there were scrambled eggs for breakfast!

When breakfast was over Juan went to work and Lorenzo went to school. Then Sarita put the dirty dishes in the sink, and said to herself: "Well, I think I will go sit in the patio a bit before I wash the dishes."

But Donato turned on the water, and as Sarita went out she heard the water splashing in the sink and had to come back to turn it off. As she reached for the faucet Donato stuck the dish cloth into her hand. And before she knew it she was washing the dishes.

When she had finished the dishes Sarita went into the living room. She found a book and started to sit down in a chair to read. But Donato snatched the cushion and his brothers tipped the chair over. Donato knocked a great cloud of dust out of the cushion.

"Dear me," said Sarita. "How did I ever upset that chair? And look at that cushion. I had no idea it was so dusty."

She put the chair back and picked up the cushion. By that time one of the duendes had snatched the book and hidden it. And then Donato put the broom into her hands.

"Mercy me!" said Sarita. "I don't remember bringing the broom in here. Well, I suppose I meant to sweep the floor."

So she started sweeping in the middle of the room. But the duendes quickly pulled the furniture around so that,

HENRY C PITZ

before she knew it, Sarita was giving the room a good sweeping.

Then she had to go ahead and sweep the rest of the house. In the bedrooms the duendes had picked up the clothes that were on the floor, and opened the windows wide. And Sarita thought that she had done it all herself. By that time she was getting pleased with herself, so she went ahead and made the beds.

Then Sarita went into the kitchen to put the broom away. And there on the sink lay a hen, freshly killed. You see, Donato had not forgotten what Lorenzo said about Sarita not cooking enough for dinner. So he had killed the hen and put it in the kitchen, and he even had a kettle of water boiling.

"Well, dear me!" said Sarita. "I don't remember killing that chicken! I must have meant to cook it for dinner. Of course, the kettle is already boiling! I'd just forgotten that I meant to cook a hen for dinner."

So Sarita cleaned the chicken and put it on to cook. And when she turned around Donato had spilled some potatoes on the floor. Sarita picked them up. And before she knew it she was paring them for dinner.

When the dinner was on to cook, Sarita felt pleased with herself. The house was nice and clean and a good dinner was cooking on the stove! Sarita had not done so much work in months. So now she really could sit down and read her book.

She went into the living room, and there was her book on the little table beside her favorite chair. But when she

sat down and reached for it, something strange happened
Instead of her book she picked up her sewing basket. And
while she was still staring at the basket and wondering how
she happened to have it in her hands, she looked down, and
there on her lap lay Lorenzo's pants!

"Dearie me!" said Sarita, "of course I meant to mend
Lorenzo's pants. Mercy! I didn't realize they were so badly
torn."

So, sitting in her nice clean house, with the chicken boil
ing on the stove, Sarita mended the pants. And she began to
sing, for all of a sudden she realized that she was very
happy.

When Lorenzo came home from school and Juan came
home from work, they saw how nice the house looked. And
they ate the fine big dinner Sarita had cooked. Lorenzo found
his pants nicely mended and hanging in his room. He put
them on and went back to school. But he forgot to tell Sarita
that he had dreamed about the duendes the night before.

When Juan started back to work he kissed Sarita goodbye
Usually he forgot to kiss her. "That was a fine dinner, Sarita,
he said, "and the house is so clean. You must have done a
lot of work. In fact I have never seen the house look so nice
Are you expecting company?"

"No," said Sarita. "No one is coming." Then she puckered
up her forehead, wondering just why she had cleaned the
house. "There was no special reason for cleaning," she said
"I suppose I just felt like working."

The next day was Saturday and Sarita fully intended to sleep late. She was still pleased with herself for doing so much work on Friday, but she had no thought of doing it every day. But on Saturday morning Donato and all his twelve brothers came in through the window again, and made Sarita get up.

When Lorenzo came out to breakfast, there was his mother sitting at the table with Juan, and both were laughing and talking. He thought how nice it was in the house when people laughed instead of quarreling.

After breakfast Juan went to work. Sarita yawned and put the dishes in the sink.

"I think I'll go out and sit in the patio a bit before I wash the dishes, Lorenzo," said Sarita. "It is just about time for the chicharron man. Go out in the street and wait for him, and buy some chicharrones and bring them to me in the patio."

Lorenzo went out, and there came the chicharron man, with the big flat basket on his head. Lorenzo bought ten centavos worth of crisp, brown chicharrones. (That is the Mexican name for "cracklings," you know.) But when he went back into the house Sarita was at the sink washing the dishes.

"Oh," said Lorenzo, "I thought you were going to sit in the patio."

"Yes, I was," Sarita seemed puzzled about it herself. "But, somehow, I just got started washing the dishes. Put the chicharrones in a dish on the table. We'll eat them later."

When Sarita finished the dishes she went to the table and put out her hand for the dish of chicharrones. But instead she picked up the dust cloth. She stared at it a minute with her brows puckered. Lorenzo could not see how it happened that she picked up the dust cloth. For he was quite sure there was nothing at all on the table except the dish of chicharrones.

"Oh, well," said Sarita with a little sigh, "I guess I meant to dust before we sit down to eat the chicharrones."

Lorenzo was puzzled. In the first place, it was very unusual for Sarita to bother about dusting and cleaning. And, in the second place, Lorenzo wondered how that dust cloth happened to be on the table. And, in the third place, he knew that Sarita was puzzled, too. So he followed her around the house and hung up clothes and helped straighten things, while she wiped the dust off all the furniture.

When she had finished the dusting Sarita started toward the kitchen with the dust cloth in her hand. She laughed and said: "Well, Lorenzo, now we will eat our chicharrones."

But just at that minute she and Lorenzo both saw that she had the broom in her hand instead of the dust cloth. Lorenzo thought he had seen the dust cloth whisk through the air, but, of course, he must have been mistaken. They both stared at the broom.

"Mamá," said Lorenzo, "I didn't see you go for the broom. What do you suppose you are doing with the broom in your hand?"

"Why, mercy me!" said Sarita crossly, "what does one

usually do with a broom? I am going to sweep the house, of course." And she went to work very fast, sweeping the house.

Lorenzo slipped out to the kitchen and looked in the closet, and, sure enough, there was the dust cloth hanging on its nail. Then he went into the living room to watch his mother sweep. But he was still puzzled.

When the sweeping was finished, they both went back to the kitchen, and Sarita put the broom into the closet. But when she turned around, there was a tub of water on the bench, and Juan's and Lorenzo's and Sarita's dirty clothes were soaking in the water. Lorenzo saw the tub at the same time, and he opened his mouth and stared.

"Well, goodness me!" said Sarita. "I'd forgotten all about those clothes!"

"Mamá, I didn't see you put those clothes in the tub!" said Lorenzo.

"Do you have to see everything?" said Sarita crossly. "I have to wash clothes if we're to keep clean, don't I?" And she went to work very fast, washing the clothes and hanging them on the line.

Lorenzo went into the living room and sat down and thought about the odd things that had been happening. Then he thought about how much work Sarita was doing. And he thought it might be a good idea to get her to mend his other pair of pants, while she was in the mood for work.

He got his pants and brought them into the living room. He could not reach Sarita's sewing basket because it was on a high shelf in the hall, so he sat down and waited. Then

Sarita came in and dropped down into her favorite chair.

"Mamá," said Lorenzo hesitantly, "you mended my other pants so nicely yesterday. But these are torn, too, and I wondered—"

Then he stopped because Sarita was frowning, and she looked tired. But just then Sarita looked down, and she had her sewing basket in her hands!

But that time Lorenzo saw what had happened. While Sarita was frowning, Lorenzo saw Donato rush across the room with the sewing basket and thrust it into her hands. Then Donato jumped up on the back of Sarita's chair and winked at Lorenzo. Then, of course, Lorenzo knew why so many queer things had been happening in that house. He winked back at Donato and began to laugh.

Then Sarita laughed, too.

"Isn't that funny?" she said. "I came in with my sewing basket in my hands, all ready to tell you to bring your pants so I can mend them. And there you sit with the pants, waiting to ask me to mend them. Isn't that funny?"

Lorenzo brought in the dish of crisp, brown chicharrones, and he and Sarita ate them while Sarita mended his pants. Lorenzo sat on the stool and chuckled to himself and watched her—or rather he watched *them*—for Donato was still perched on the back of Sarita's chair. Every little while he would lean down and whisper in her ear. Then Sarita would look at Lorenzo and smile, but she did not say anything.

Now, of course, you understand that Sarita did not know

anything about Donato. So when he whispered to her, she thought she was just hearing her own thoughts.

"Lorenzo is a very good boy," whispered Donato, and Sarita thought she was thinking it herself. So she looked at Lorenzo and smiled.

"He is really a very handsome boy and a son to be proud of," whispered Donato. And Sarita thought she was thinking it herself.

"But his clothes are very ragged," whispered Donato. "I should take better care of my son. Now that my house is nice and clean, I see how ragged he is."

Then Sarita put her sewing in her lap and looked hard at Lorenzo. His clothes certainly were ragged, and he had not been washing properly behind his ears. But she was proud of him.

"Lorenzo," said Sarita suddenly, and she laughed like a little girl who has thought of something delightful, "get my purse so I can give you some money. Then I want you to run to the market place and buy some manta. I'm going to make you a brand new pair of pants. If you hurry I can finish them today. Juan says we are going to the fiesta tonight, and I'll have them made in time for you to wear them."

Lorenzo jumped up and threw his arms about Sarita's neck and gave her a big kiss. Over her shoulder he looked up at Donato and whispered, "Thank you."

Donato winked at him and leaped off the chair onto the table. He grabbed a piece of crisp, brown chicharron, and flashed across the room toward the window. Lorenzo saw a blur of bright green caps outside the window. Then it was gone.

Lorenzo hugged Sarita again and started for the door. There he paused.

"Mamá, do you believe there really are duendes?" he asked.

"Duendes?" said Sarita. "Mercy me, child! I haven't time to think of duendes. I have too much work to do. If people want to be happy they must keep their homes nice, and that means work. I have better things to do than think about duendes."

"Well, I believe in them, Mamá."

"That's all right for children," said Sarita. "But I am much too busy to think about duendes. Now run along and get that manta, or your new pants won't be finished in time for the fiesta."

And Lorenzo knew that now he had a tremendous, wonderful secret!

Pancho and the Duendes

THIS is the story of a little boy named Pancho who grew to be an old man on a coffee plantation in Mexico. Now that Pancho is an old man, he likes to sit out in the sun in the afternoon and tell stories to Carmen and Petra and Lolita. These are three little girls, who are still little, and who still live on that same coffee plantation.

One day Pancho was sitting in the sun in the patio and

the three little girls came and asked him to tell them a story.

"What shall I tell you about?" asked Pancho.

"Tell us about when you were a little boy!" cried Lolita.

"No, tell us about when you lived in the town!" said Carmen.

"Oh, no, Pancho! Tell us about the duendes!" begged Petra.

"That is three stories," said Pancho, "but I can tell them all at once."

For you see, the truth is that the duendes had a great deal to do with Pancho's life when he was a little boy. And they certainly had a lot to do with him when he lived in town, which was only one year out of his whole long life. The duendes, as you probably know, are elves. They are very mischievous little people and their doings are often blamed on the carelessness of children. There are very few people in the world who can see the duendes, and for that reason most people do not believe in them. But Pancho learned to see them when he was a little boy.

Pancho's mother was the cook on the big coffee planta-tion, so Pancho knew that he would work there, too, when he grew up. Of course he had to go to school when he was little. But after school he used to go down to the woods by the river, or sometimes out into the thick groves of coffee trees, where he lay on his back and watched the birds, and listened to the songs the wind sang in the trees. And some-times he would climb high in the big mango tree in the back garden and pretend he was marooned on a desert island.

That was when he got acquainted with the duendes. For the duendes live in the woods and fields, and go into towns and into people's houses only when they want to play jokes on someone.

One day Pancho was sitting up in the mango tree, pretending he was signalling to a distant ship. He wanted to take off his shirt to wave, but he was afraid his mother might call him and he would not have time to put it on again. It would be pretty hard to explain to the grown-ups why he was up in a tree with his shirt off, so he just waved and pretended he had his shirt in his hand.

All of a sudden he found that he did have something in his hand! But it wasn't a shirt. It was a funny little green cap. It was very small, much too small for Pancho, and although it was quite sturdy it seemed to be woven of cobwebs. Pancho stared at the little cap and wondered where on earth it had come from. Then while he stared straight at it, it was suddenly jerked out of his hand and disappeared right before his eyes.

Pancho was so surprised that he forgot to hold to the limb on which he was sitting, and he lost his balance and fell. Down, down through the branches, bumping from limb to limb, he fell right out of the mango tree and landed on the hard ground. It knocked the breath out of him, and for a minute he just lay there and gasped.

"Goodness me, Pancho, I am sorry," said a little voice right beside him. "I never dreamed you would let go and fall, or I wouldn't have played that joke on you!"

Pancho opened his eyes and looked around, but there was no one there. Then he saw a tiny green cap bobbing in the air beside him. He rubbed his eyes and looked again. And then he saw a tiny little man, wearing the green cap. He was an odd-looking little man about a foot tall, with a wrinkled old face and slim legs, and he was wearing a little green jacket to match the funny green cap.

"Well," said Pancho, "you must be a duende."

"Yes, I'm Goyo, a duende. I do hope you aren't hurt?"

"Well, bless my eyebrows!" said Pancho. "I've never seen a duende before."

"I know," said Goyo. "You see we only just found out that you are the sort of person who can be allowed to see us."

"Oh," said Pancho. "What sort of person am I?"

"You are a good little boy, with imagination and understanding, even though you are rather lazy and misbehave in school," said Goyo. "I say, I do hope you aren't hurt?"

"Well, bless my ears!" said Pancho.

After that Pancho used to see the duendes very often, and he got to be very good friends with Goyo and all the tribe of duendes that lived in the coffee groves. But as he grew older he could not see them so often because he had to help his mother with the work. Then when he was a fairly big boy, he left school and went to work himself.

But by that time he had learned so much about the work inside the house, from helping his mother and the maids, that the people who owned the plantation did not want him to work at picking the coffee and taking care of the horses. They wanted him to work in the house. And after a few more years Pancho was the mayordomo of the household. (*Mayordomo* is Spanish, and means "chief servant." But in our country he would have been called a butler.)

So for a long time Pancho worked in the big house on the coffee plantation. He served the meals and directed the other servants, and saw that the house was kept nice and clean. In the afternoon, when he was not busy, he still went out into the coffee groves and talked with the duendes.

That was long before Petra and Carmen and Lolita were born. In fact, their father, Gabriel, was only a small boy then. And he used to go out in the coffee groves and down by the river with Pancho sometimes. Once or twice he, too, had seen the duendes, but he was never quite so sure of it as Pancho was.

Then Pancho began dreaming about the town. When he went there to a fiesta he thought it was very exciting. He decided that he would like to get work at one of the big houses in town, so he could live there all the time. When they heard this the people who lived on the coffee plantation were very sad, for they liked Pancho and did not want him to leave them. But since that was what he wanted to do, they promised to help him get work in town. Gabriel wept, and Pancho felt sad about that. But he still wanted to go to town.

When Pancho was all ready to leave he went down by the river and sat for a long time, because he wanted to see

Goyo once more before he went away, for he was quite sure
that Goyo would never come to the town. When he had been
sitting still for a long time, his hat suddenly flew off his head
and leaped up and hung on a branch of a tree. He looked up
and, sure enough, there was Goyo, laughing at him from the
midst of the thick green leaves.

"I've come to say goodbye, Goyo," said Pancho. "I'm going to live in town."

"What on earth for?" said Goyo. "Town is no place to
live."

"It is more exciting to live in town," said Pancho.

"You are very foolish," said Goyo angrily. "You'll never
like it. You belong right here."

"Yes, I will like it," said Pancho. "I'm going to work in
a big house in town, and have a new life."

"You'll be sorry," said Goyo. "Wait and see!"

"Now, listen—" Pancho began.

Then he stopped and stared around him because Goyo
was gone. He looked everywhere but there was no sign of
Goyo. He called and called, but Goyo did not answer him.
So Pancho climbed up in the tree and got his hat. Then
he thought he heard Goyo laugh, but he could not see him.
And when he called there was no answer. So he went back
to the house and got his things, and went to town to live in
a big house and work for a new family.

In a way, it was nice in town. There were lots of fiestas,
and Pancho was invited to quite a few little parties on his

one day off. But he did miss Gabriel and the coffee groves and Goyo.

At first everything went along splendidly. Pancho learned how the new family liked their house run, and how they liked their meals served. He was a very good worker, so the new family liked him. Then, all of a sudden, everything began going wrong. The first thing was terribly embarrassing. There was company for dinner, and Pancho was very proud because the table looked so nice. When everyone was seated, Pancho carried in the big bowl of soup to set beside the mistress's place, so that she could serve her guests. But just as he started to set the soup on the table, someone pushed his arm and he dropped the bowl and it upset, and the hot soup went all over the mistress's lovely evening dress.

Pancho felt ashamed and began mopping up the soup with a napkin. Then he leaned over and whispered to the mistress: "I'm sorry, Señora, but someone pushed my arm."

"Ridiculous!" hissed the mistress. "No one could have pushed your arm."

Pancho looked around and there was no one there except the guests seated at the table. And certainly they could not have done it. Just the same, he had felt someone push his arm. He saw a queer flash of green at one of the windows just then, but was so disturbed that he did not think anything about it.

After that, almost every day Pancho spilled something

when he was serving the dinner. He was very careful, looking behind him when he carried in the dishes, and there was never anyone near him. And yet suddenly someone would bump his arm and make him spill something. The mistress was angry with him almost every day.

Then it happened that each morning all the lamps in the house would be found lighted, except the lamps in the bedrooms. Even the tall candles on the dining table would be lighted, and the candle grease would be dripping on the beautiful table. The mistress was very angry about this, too. And Pancho was worried about it. Each night he went over the house, making sure to blow out all the lamps, and to lock the doors and see that everything was in order. But in spite of that, in the morning all the lamps were lighted again. Pancho could not think how it happened!

So one day the mistress told him he was so careless that she did not want him to work for her any more, and he must leave. Pancho packed his things and set out to find another job. He still had the letter the people on the coffee plantation had given him, saying what a good servant he was. And after a while he found another family that wanted a good mayordomo, and he went to work for them.

At first everything went along splendidly. All the other servants liked Pancho, and he was so careful about his work and so pleasant, that the family liked him, too. Pancho thought that all the bad luck he had had at the other house was finished now and that at last he was going to enjoy working in town.

But Pancho had been working in the new house only a month when strange things began happening again. The first trouble was that thing of someone bumping his arm when he was serving. He spilled soup on the mistress and coffee on the master. And he dropped a big hot fish down the back of a very fat lady guest. All at one meal! The mistress was very angry. And after that, almost every day Pancho spilled something when he was serving.

Then again it happened that every morning all the lamps in the house were lighted, except only in the bedrooms. The mistress was very angry about this, too. And Pancho was worried. At night he would go through the house after everyone was in bed, and make sure that all the lamps were out and the doors locked. He even put the tall candles on the floor in the corner, so they would not light themselves and drip on the table. But in spite of that, in the morning all the lamps were lighted, and the candles were back on the table, dripping on the lovely cloth. And then Pancho began getting up very early, so that he could go around and blow out the lamps before the mistress got up. But even so, lots of times, she knew what had happened.

Then one morning Pancho got up and found his own room in a terrible mess! His clothes were piled in the middle of the floor, the chest of drawers was turned to face the wall, the chairs were upside down, and the window curtains torn down. He did not have time to straighten things up just then, because he had to hurry upstairs to see about the lamps. In the afternoon, when he could have rested, he had to clean up his own room. After that every morning his room was in a mess.

But that wasn't the worst. One day the mistress was having guests for tea. Pancho saw that the sala was nicely arranged with fresh flowers, and that there was a fine white cloth on the tea table. The mistress was still in her room dressing when the guests arrived. Pancho let them in and took them to the sala. But when he opened the door, he almost fainted. The flowers were scattered on the floor, the white cloth was rumpled, and every chair in the sala was turned to the wall! Pancho was horrified and so were the guests. And just then the mistress walked in and was the most horrified of all. She was very angry with Pancho.

But this time Pancho knew what had happened. For, while he stood there staring at the disordered room, he heard a soft chuckle of laughter and saw a dozen shadowy little figures with funny green caps, rush for the window. The only thing that surprised him was that he had not thought of them sooner.

The mistress took the guests into the patio, while Pancho and Maria, the maid, cleaned up the room again. And all the time Pancho was muttering angrily. He had thought the duendes were his friends, and yet this was the way they treated him. But he thought that now that he knew it was the duendes who had been making the trouble, he would watch closely and try to keep them from bothering him any more.

But after that things grew worse. You see, the trouble was that Pancho could not see the duendes unless they wanted him to, so there wasn't much he could do about stopping them. They still mussed up his room and lighted the lamps and made him spill things at the table. And almost every morning he found all the chairs in the sala turned to the wall.

But that wasn't all. If he walked behind the cook in the kitchen, the duendes would suddenly bump her arm and make her spill something. And she would think that it was Pancho and be angry with him. If he walked past one of the maids, the duendes would grab her apron string and untie it. And she would think that Pancho did it. It became so bad that almost everyone in the house was cross at him most of the time.

One morning when he got up, he found his room in a mess, and straightened it all up. Just as he finished and had it looking nice and neat, the mistress knocked at his door. She was up early and wanted to talk to him about the house-cleaning.

"How nice your room looks, Pancho," said the mistress. "I am glad to see you still keep it clean, even if you have grown so careless about serving."

Pancho went upstairs with her and began to do his work. But everything went wrong that morning. The cook dropped a big bowl of rice and broke the bowl, scattering the rice all over the floor. Pancho was right beside her and she said he had grabbed her arm. She felt him jerk it, she said. And Maria's apron flew off into the kettle of soup. She said Pancho did it, for he was right beside her and she felt him jerk it off.

At dinner just when Pancho had almost reached the table with a big bowl of soup, the duendes pushed the bowl from the bottom and it tipped and poured the soup over Pancho's white coat and down onto the floor.

"Mop it up," said the mistress wearily. "And let Maria serve the rice, while you go down to change your coat."

Now Pancho was very angry with the duendes. He went down to change his coat. And there was his room in a terrible mess again! It wasn't enough that they messed it up at night. Now they were messing it in the daytime, too. He did not have time to straighten things then, so he put on a clean coat and went back upstairs to finish serving dinner.

Things were still bad. When he carried in the desserts, one of the custards hopped off the tray and fell to the floor. And he spilled coffee on the clean white tablecloth. The mistress didn't say a word. She just looked at him and seemed very tired.

After dinner the mistress went to sit in the patio, and she sent for Pancho to come out there so that she could talk to him.

"Pancho," she said, "we all like you, but you have become such a bad servant that I must send you away. We cannot stand your accidents and your carelessness any longer."

"But, Señora," said Pancho, "I'm not careless. It's—it's— well, perhaps I'd better just tell you the truth."

"It is always best to tell the truth, Pancho."

"I'm afraid you won't believe me, but—it's the duendes, Señora."

"The duendes?"

"Yes. You know what duendes are?"

"Of course. But there are no such things as duendes."

"Then how do you know what they are?"

"Everyone knows what duendes are supposed to be. But they are not real—just imaginary."

"No, Señora," said Pancho stubbornly. "I've seen the duendes lots of times. It is they who bump my arms when I am carrying dishes. They light the lamps at night. And they change the furniture around."

The mistress laughed. "Well, Pancho, you'll have to think of a better excuse than that. I've never seen duendes, so I do not believe in them."

Then Pancho had an idea. Perhaps he could convince her it was the duendes.

"Señora," he said, "this morning you saw my room and you know that I had cleaned it up and it was nice and neat?"

"Yes, Pancho, it looked very nice."

"Well," said Pancho, "no one has been in my room since then. Yet when I went down to change my coat after I spilled the soup—I mean when the duendes spilled the soup on me— the room was all messed up again. Doesn't that prove it was the duendes?"

"I know no one has been in your room. And you were not down there long enough to mess it up, even if you had wanted to do such a foolish thing. But I have not seen the room messed up."

"Will you come with me and see the room, Señora? Then

when you see what they have done there, you will believe
that it is the duendes."

"All right," said the mistress. "I'll come and see it. I know
you did not mess it up yourself, so if it is disordered, perhaps
there are duendes."

At this point in Pancho's story the three little girls
squirmed and bounced on their three little stools.

"And she believed you then!" cried Petra. "When she got
to your room and saw the mess, she believed in the duendes,
didn't she?"

"No," said Pancho.

"But that proved it!" shouted Lolita. "She said it would
prove it, if the room was messed up."

"Well, you see," said Pancho, "when I opened the door
of my room, I heard a gale of chuckling duende laughter.
And I saw a dozen duendes, quite clearly, with their little
green coats and funny green caps, leaping out through the
window."

"Well, that proved it," shrieked Carmen. "Did she see
them too?"

"No," said Pancho. "She couldn't see them, and they knew
it."

"But anyway, there was the messy room," said Petra.

"No," said Pancho, "those naughty duendes had gone
back and straightened everything up. The room was clean
and neat as could be. Everything was as it had been when
the mistress saw it in the morning."

"Then did she let you stay, because it was nice and clean?" asked Carmen.

"No," said Pancho. "She said I was not only a bad servant, but I made up foolish stories about duendes. So she made me leave."

"So then you came back home, didn't you?" said Petra.

"Yes," said Pancho. "I came back home. And I was very glad to see Gabriel again and to be back with my friends. Goyo said, 'I told you so,' but it didn't matter."

"Weren't you cross at Goyo for being so mean to you?" asked Carmen.

"No," said Pancho. "Sometimes the duendes have to be pretty rough to make us stop being foolish. I might never have come back home to the coffee groves, if it hadn't been for the duendes. And that would have been terrible."

Glossary

a *as in* father; e *as in* prey; i *as in* police; o *as in* hope; u *as in* rule; h *is always silent;* j *has sound of* h; ll *is pronounced like* y; ñ *as* ny *as in* canyon; x *is pronounced sometimes like* s *and sometimes like* h; but the Indians always make it sound like sh.

The nice thing about Spanish and Indian words is that they are always pronounced exactly as they are spelled. The only thing that may be difficult is to learn to pronounce some of the Indian names in which t and l come together. You just pronounce the two letters, tl —not tel nor til, but just tl, as though you start to say t and change it to an l. Try it.

In the following words we have marked the syllable to be accented. Accent that syllable and run the other syllables in smoothly.

abuela (ahboo-él-ah)—grandmother.
adobe (ah-dó-bay)—sun-dried bricks.
allá (ah-yáh)—there or yonder.
Anáhuac (Ahn-áh-ooahk)—the ancient Indian name for the Valley of Mexico. It means Valley of Water.
blanco (bláhn-ko)—white.
brujo (bróo-ho)—a male witch. A lady witch is a bruja. The dog in the story just had a strong name.

burro—you know how to pronounce this one, but please roll the rr.

burrito (boor-ée-to)—a little donkey.

calle (káh-yay)—street.

caramba (kah-ráhm-ba)—just an exclamation, about as strong as gosh.

chicharrones (chee-chah-rón-es)—the plural of chicharron, which is just a chitterling or crackling. They are delicious.

Chucha (Chóo-cha)—the nickname for Jesusa (Hay-sóos-ah), a girl's name. A boy named Jesus (Hay-sóos) would be called Chucho.

cochino (ko-chéen-o)—a pig or even a hog.

cochinito (ko-cheen-ée-to)—a little pig.

Concha (kón-cha)—concha really means shell, but when it is used as a name it is the nickname for Concepción. There are lots of girls named Concepción.

conejo (kon-áy-ho)—rabbit.

Cuautla (koo-ah-óot-la)—the name of a very nice town.

Cupatitzio (koo-pah-téet-see-o)—the name of a river. It is a Tarascan word and means clear and swift.

duende (doo-énd-ay)—elf.

fiesta (fee-és-tah)—any kind of a party.

Goyo (just as it is spelled)—the nickname for Gregorio or Gregory.

guarache (ooah-ráh-chay)—sometimes it is spelled huaracha, because the g is just barely sounded and most people do not bother to sound it at all. It means sandal. It is an Indian word, but everybody uses it.

Guillermo (g *as in* good. Gee-yér-mo)—the Spanish for William.

hacienda (ah-see-énd-a)—a big farm.

Ixtlaccihuatl (eesht-lahk-see-watl)—all syllables equal in accent. This is an Indian word that means The Sleeping Lady. It is the name given to a lovely mountain.

leon (lay-ón)—lion.

Luz (lóos)—the word for light. It is often used as a girl's name.

machete (mah-cháy-tay)—a huge knife.

machincuepa (mah-cheen-kooáp-a)—a somersault.

maguey (mah-gáy)—the aloe or century plant.

Mali (Máh-lee)—just a name.

mango (máhn-go)—the most delicious fruit you ever ate.

manta (máhn-ta)—unbleached muslin.

mantequilla (mahn-tay-kée-yah)—butter.

Marina (Mah-rée-nah)—the Spanish for Marian.

Mateo (Mah-táy-o)—the Spanish for Matthew.

mayordomo (mah-yor-dó-mo)—butler or head servant.

mazaquate (mah-sah-kooáh-tay)—a huge snake of the jungle country, called a boa constrictor in English. This is an Indian word.

Miguel (g *as in* good. Mee-gél)—the Spanish of Michael.

niño (néen-yo)—a little boy, or boy baby. A little girl is a niña.

oro—that is too easy; it means gold.

Paco (Páh-ko)—this is a nickname for Francisco, which is Spanish for Francis or Frank.

Pancho (Páhn-cho)—another nickname for Francisco.

Papantla (Pah-páhnt-lah)—the name of a town in the hot country. It is a Totonac word and means the rich land.

pasa (páh-sah)—this is the present tense of pasar, which means to pass or to happen. So when we say "que pasa" it means what is happening or what goes on.

Pedro (Páy-dthro)—that d sound is a cross between d and th. See if you can say it. Pedro is Spanish for Peter.

Petra (Páy-trah)—this is the feminine of Pedro. If we named girls Peter this is what it would be in Spanish.

Pepe (Páy-pay)—this really means Joe, because it is the nickname of José which means Joseph.

Popocatepetl (Po-po-kah-táy-petl)—remember about that tl? Pronounce the last syllable like petal with the *a* left out. This word is mispronounced by foreigners more consistently than any place name in Mexico. It is a Nahuatl word and means The Smoking Mountain. It is the name of a beautiful mountain peak.

pues (poo-es)—run it all together as one syllable. This means well when used as an exclamation. If you say you are feeling well, you use bien, but if you say "well, let's go" you use pues for well.

que (kay)—what.

quexquen (káysh-kayn)—this is a Totonac word and is the name of a special little shawl the Indian women wear.

quien (key-én)—who.

Raul (Rah-óol)—a boy's name. No English equivalent.

sabe (sáh-bay)—the present tense of *saber,* which means to know. So *sabe* means knows.

sacate (sah-káh-tay)—any kind of fodder or heavy grass.

sala (sáh-la)—the living room or parlor.

Salvador (Sahl-vah-dór)—this means Saviour, but it is often used as a name for boys.

Tarascan (Tah-ráhs-kan)—the name of one of the Indian nations, or of their people, who still live in Mexico.

Tecolutla (Tay-ko-lóot-la)—the name of a Totonac Indian town in the state of Vera Cruz.

Tenochtitlan (Tay-nóch-teet-láhn)—this is the ancient Indian name of what is now Mexico City. It is made up of three Nahuatl words and means "place where a cactus grows from a stone."

Tepetl (Táy-petl)—the Nahuatl word for mountain.

Ticho (Tée-cho)—this is really Pat because it is the nickname for Patricio which means Patrick.

tlacuache (tlah-kooáh-chay)—the Indian name of a little animal related to the raccoon. He is only found in Mexico, so there is no other name for him.

tortilla (tor-tée-yah)—unleavened corn cakes.

Totonaca (To-to-náh-kah)—the name of an Indian people. They live in the state of Vera Cruz.

Uruapan (oor-ooáh-pahn)—the name of a lovely village. In the Tarascan language it means "place of water."

venado (ve-náh-do)—a male deer. A doe is a venada.

Xochitl (só-chitl is the way the Mexicans pronounce it, but the Indians call it shó-chitl)—this is the Nahuatl word for flower.

yolo (yó-lo)—the Nahuatl word for heart. So Yoloxochitl means "Heartflower."

zopilote (so-pee-ló-tay)—buzzard.

zorro (sór-ro)—fox.

A NOTE ON THE TYPE

The text of this book is set in Caledonia, a Linotype face designed by W. A. Dwiggins. The bold type used in the chapter headings, etc., is Bernhard Modern Bold, made by the American Type Founders Company. Both Caledonia and Bernhard Modern Bold belong to the family of printing-types called "modern face," a term used to mark the change in style of type-letters that occurred about 1800.

The book was composed, printed, and bound by H. WOLFF, *New York.*